Sophie

&

Carter

By Chelsea Fine

Praise for the *Sophie & Carter*

Best Contemporary Book of 2011 (Book Twirps)
Best Indie Book of the Year (My Overstuffed Bookshelf)
Top Ten Characters of 2011 "Carter" (The Autumn Review)
Best Books of 2011 (Kate's Tales of Books and Bands)
Best Female Lead in YA (Lovely Lit)
2012 Novella Finalist (DABWAHA)

""I literally could not put this book down! This is a tender and emotional love story focused on two teens handed much more from life than they might be able to handle without one another."
(Katy Brady)

"I've walked away from books twice as long and didn't feel as connected as I did to these characters. I laughed, I cried and I loved these characters' guts!"
(Tasha, Goodreads)

"A glimpse into...harsh realities, and the impact a 'few peaceful moments on a porch swing and an understanding friend' can have on a person's existence."
(Kindle Obsessed, Book Reviewer)

"Sophie and Carter have to be two of the best characters I have read this year. They were so real and raw and just amazing. In fact, this book is amazing."
(My Guilty Obsession, Book Reviewer)

"A boy-and-girl-next-door young adult story unlike anything I've ever read...."
(The Whispered Word, Book Reviewer)

Also by Chelsea Fine

Anew

Awry

And Coming Soon

Avow

Sophie & Carter

Chelsea Fine

Firefall Publishing

This is a work of fiction. All of the characters, organizations, and events portrayed in this novel are either productions of the author's imagination or are used fictitiously.

SOPHIE & CARTER

Copyright © 2011 by Chelsea Fine

All rights reserved.

No part of this publication may be reproduced, stored in a retrieval system or transmitted in any form or by any methods, photocopying, scanning, electronic or otherwise, except as permitted by notation in the volume or under Sections 107 or 108 of the 1976 United States Copyright Act, without the prior written permission of the author.

ISBN 9780988585911

Contact the author via
www.TheArchersofAvalon.com
www.ChelseaFineBooks.com

Published by
Firefall Publishing
Phoenix, AZ

Cover design by Jason Crye

*For my amazing mom,
who always believes in me*

SOPHIE

I'm late for English.

This is not uncommon. I have a tendency to dawdle at lunch. *Dawdle* is a word my mom would use when she wanted to call me lazy. I never use it out loud, but I use it a lot in my head.

So I'm late.

I'm running through the halls (well, let's be honest here, I'm not running. I'm walking. Casually. English doesn't excite me, so I refuse to break a sweat to get there) thinking about what my excuse for being tardy will be, and I see *him*.

Carter Jax.

He makes my heart stop, he makes my breaths shallow, he makes me want to sing.

I know, super corny, right? But agh, it's true.

He's not the most popular guy in school. He's not the hottest guy to ever live. But to me, he's everything.

I'm somewhat disgusted at myself for thinking such dramatic, girlie thoughts. But I can't help myself. He rocks my world.

You know how parents always say things like, "If all your friends jumped off a cliff, would you jump too?"

Well if Carter jumped off a cliff, I wouldn't just jump off after him. I'd throw myself over the ledge and dive toward the earth below so I could catch up with him and hold his hand while we plummeted to our deaths.

Yeah.

I'm that much of a sicko.

So anyway, Carter's in the hallway, looking at me with his quirky smile and an eyebrow raised. He's wearing his faded jeans and blue t-shirt like he just stepped out of a magazine ad. And he easily could have.

Broad shoulders, square jaw, piercing gray eyes…everything about his appearance is picture-perfect.

Everything except the scars.

I feel my heart squeeze in my chest and immediately redirect my thoughts to happier things.

Like root canals.

We walk toward one another slowly. It's just the two of us. No other students are around, which is rare. We don't typically run into one another during school—at least not when we're alone. And that's how we like it.

We pretend we don't know each other at school. It's a silent understanding we've had for years. It keeps our school lives separate from our home lives and keeps us from going crazy. School is our escape.

As we near each other I absently inhale, welcoming the familiar scent of Carter's soap. It smells like the ocean.

I've never been to the ocean, let alone breathed it in, but in my mind the ocean smells like Carter. Therefore, I love the ocean.

"Late again?" Carter smiles. "What's your excuse today, Sophie?"

I love it when he says my name.

He knows me well, so he knows I'm always late for English.

"I'm thinking about blaming a faulty toilet in the girls' room." I say, as I tuck my hair behind my ear. I sound normal because I'm good at acting normal around Carter.

He smiles.

I melt.

The conversation goes on. "I wish I was in your English class. I'd love to watch your teacher lecture you on punctuality day after day..," he rolls his eyes, "...after day. Poor guy."

I smile back, because any other response (like jumping into his arms and kissing him) would be stupid. "Yeah, well, AP English is for us smarties. Aren't you supposed to be in class right now too? Like maybe Womanizing 101?"

Carter's not the most popular guy in school, but he's got some serious swagger.

I hate this about him.

I also love this about him.

"You know I don't need any classes on women. I've got them all figured out." He gives a cocky smile and I narrow my eyes at him, twitching my lips so I don't smile.

He's not cocky at all, but like I said, we pretend at school. We're completely different kids at school. We're normal kids.

"Really? Figured out all the anatomical differences between our genders finally?" I tease him because I can. He lets me.

"Ah, you know very well I figured all that out years ago."

No actually, I don't *know very well*. But I have ears and my ears *know very well*.

"Women," he begins, puffing out his chest and speaking with authority, "are simple. Just compliment them all the time and they'll think you're awesome."

This, I know for a fact, is not true. Because Carter has never complimented me. And I think he's awesome.

I'm stupid. I don't care.

"And men," I counter, stepping closer because when we're at school he always shifts uncomfortably when I'm near, "are weak. Because all you have to do is pout your lips and bat your lashes and they'll do anything you say."

I bat my eyelashes a few times and hold my gaze steady as he tries not to make any expression. I know him so well.

"Careful Sophie." His voice is so low I can feel it brushing my waist. "Keep saying things like that and I'm not going to believe you're as innocent as you look."

He's knows all about me, so his words are empty.

We stare at each other without moving. Our breaths are silent and I'm sure my heartbeat is echoing up and down the hallway. I don't want to break our gaze, so I don't give in. Neither does Carter, which is fine with me. I'd gladly stay locked in his gaze until I died of starvation.

See? Sicko.

These rare encounters at school, when no one is around, let us act like every other high school senior. Flirting, loitering in the hallway, breathing in each others pulse…just like normal teenagers.

But in real life, I never feel like a teenager. Which is why I wish moments like these would never end.

A defeated sigh tumbles down the hallway in our direction. "Can't you kids get to class on time like all the other students?" It's our principal, Mr. Wesley. He sounds weary, but we know he's not mad. He's all talk.

"No," We both say at the same time as we turn our attention to him. We don't look at one another. Saying things at the same time is nothing new to us.

Mr. Wesley sighs and shakes his head. "Right. Okay, then. Get to class."

He walks away without looking back to make sure we're headed to class. But our moment is over, so we're parting.

"See you later?" Carter asks.

It's the hitch in his voice, the hopefulness I hear, that breaks my heart and completes me at the same time.

I wink, because it's not weird for me to wink at him.

"Of course." I say. Because I'm a sure thing.

We've never had sex. Or made out. Or kissed.

But when it comes to me being there for him and blindly holding my heart out to him, then I'm a sure thing.

And he knows it.

And he's careful with it.

And that's why Carter Jax is my best friend.

CARTER

Sophie and I don't walk home from school together. We never have. But we live next door to one another on Penrose Street.

Right next door.

Sophie usually walks twenty feet ahead of me on our way home. I'm used to this and it feels comfortable. On days when Sophie stays home sick or...whatever, it feels wrong. I walk home alone and I can never seem to get there fast enough.

Today she's here, though, walking in front of me. Not acknowledging me, which is our unspoken understanding. We act like we don't know each other around our friends.

It keeps things simple. It keeps reality out.

I shove my hands in my pockets, my eyes falling on the familiar cracks in the sidewalk beneath me. The wind carries scents of the neighborhood up to my nose as I walk. Dirt...rubber...grass...even a little garbage, meet my nostrils reminding me of home.

We don't live in the nicest part of town, but it could be worse.

The houses are small and crooked, but the trees are large and stand up tall. Large oaks stretch their canopies over the leaky roofs and peeling paint of the homes below, keeping the secrets in and the sunlight out.

Not that sunlight would help any.

I bring my head up and survey the street. A long time ago the neighborhood was probably pretty nice…back before the pavement cracked and lifted, and the streetlights hung at dangerous angles. I'm sure there was a time when Penrose Street was probably an ideal place to walk your dog or have a barbeque.

Not anymore, though.

The only dogs in the neighborhood are strays, and barbeques are something I've only seen on TV.

A breeze floats through the air, softly lifting Sophie's hair from her shoulders. I catch a glimpse of her profile as her hair rises and smile to myself. Sophie has no idea how attractive she is.

At school she walks around guarded, paying no mind to the teenage Neanderthals vying for her attention. Kids don't understand why she's so quiet and uninterested. They don't know anything about her.

But I do.

A leaf falls from one of the tall oaks and brushes against Sophie's arm before falling to the ground. My eyes stay on her as we near our houses.

I like to watch her walk—and not in a sexual way. Don't get me wrong, she's got a nice butt. Actually, she's got nice...everything.

But there's something about how she walks; how she holds herself high and keeps her head straight and knows where she's going. It's beautiful.

I've been watching her walk home twenty feet ahead of me since the third grade. That's when she moved in next door.

We were nine, my life was hell, and she was new.

She was also the reason I went to school. Or got up in the morning. Or kept breathing.

The promise of Sophie.

She drops a piece of paper on the ground without stopping.

It's for me. It's how we talk on our walk home.

I keep my pace steady, even though I want to race to where the paper scrap fell and retrieve it like a possessive hound.

My feet finally reach where her note landed and I bend to pick it up, barely slowing my momentum.

I open the small folded note. It's covered in smiley faces. Of course.

Stop staring at my butt.

I smile.

Like I said, she's got a great butt. But right now I'm not staring at it.

She knows I'm not staring at it.

No. I'm staring at her skinny fingers, wrapped like magnets around the strap of her book bag. Her knuckles are white and her forearm is flexed. She's tense.

We're almost home. This is the worst part of the day—for both of us.

I shove her note in my pocket and take a deep breath. We're each at our driveways now. Sophie doesn't look over at me or say goodbye. I don't wave or look at her either.

Because this is the beginning of the end of our day. This is when things go wrong.

This is why she dropped me a note.

Because she knows, and I know, that we both need a little levity before we walk into our homes after school.

Homes.

They're not really homes. More like houses where we sleep.

Where we eat—if we're lucky. Where we cry and fight.

Where we bleed and break. Where we cower and scream.

Where we give up. Where we sigh.

Where we barely survive.

I know this because our houses are only ten feet apart. Her bedroom window faces mine. Her kitchen window faces mine.

We see everything that happens to each other. It's terrible, intrusive, and embarrassing.

It's also the reason Sophie Hartman is my best friend.

SOPHIE

My mom's a prostitute. She calls herself a call girl or an escort, but really she's a hooker.

I resent her.

Not because of her profession. In fact, her job has kept food on our table and clothes on our backs for years. She's beautiful and sexy. I'm sure she's good at what she does.

No, I resent her because sometime over the last few years, she's become a drug addict.

I have three younger siblings. I think we all have different fathers, although my mom swears we're all the offspring of some "really cool guy" named Amos.

Amos is a stupid name. I hope she's lying.

Either way, this Amos guy hasn't been around for, oh, ever, so it's just me and the 'Littles' (as I like to call them).

My mom, in her selfish, drug-induced haze, rarely comes home. Sometimes I doubt she remembers where home is. The Littles don't ask where she is anymore because they're used to her disappearing for months at a time. It's been this way for years.

We'll go as long as possible without money, but then the landlord starts calling and I have to track down my mom.

I call Pete, my mom's manager (aka: pimp), when I need to find her. Pete's a slimeball—no surprise there—but he always puts me in contact with my mom.

She'll get on the phone and laugh and cry and sing and tell me how much she loves all us kids and how she's so sorry she's been away for a few days (try a few months) and that she'll be home soon (maybe Christmas?).

I bite my tongue throughout the call because I know it's the drugs. I know deep down my sober mom does love us and hates that she's being so selfish.

I listen and say all the right things: *I love you too, we miss you too, yes, the Littles are doing good in school and remember who you are.* Finally, before we hang up, I'll ask my mother for money.

She'll get all emotional and fill up with guilt and promise me the moon and the stars.

I don't want the solar system. I want to buy bread and keep from being evicted.

It'll take a few days, but eventually money will wind up in my checking account. I'll pay all the bills, cry myself to sleep, and hope that we can make it through the next few months without needing more money from her.

The Littles don't know any of this. They think our mom travels a lot on business. They're used to me being the parent and making dinner, tucking them in, setting house rules, and taking care of them when they're sick.

I'm used to it too.

It makes me feel dry inside.

Because without a mom, there's no one left to take care of me.

Except Carter.

He's why I can handle things like potty-training a three-year-old, grounding a nine-year-old, and tutoring an eleven-year-old.

The Littles are bigger now. Chloe's six, Abram's twelve, and Michael is fourteen.

I'm eighteen. I feel like I'm forty.

Now that we're all in school during the day, I don't have to worry about paying for childcare, which is a big relief.

And now that I'm legally an adult, I can pick the Littles up from school if they get sick or—in Michael's case—get in a fight. Thankfully, Michael's freshman year of high school has been incident-free.

It didn't used to be this easy.

I walk inside my house and make sure my mom's not there. A few times over the years, she's come home to "surprise" us all, and it's usually a train wreck. I try to prevent any disasters from crashing into the Littles. Like track marks up and down Mom's arms, or boyfriends named Bubba who smell like blood and urine.

It's lousy.

I get home twenty minutes before the bus comes with the Littles. It's the easiest part of my day. It's twenty minutes of being a teenager in my house.

Once the Littles get home, I'm mom. I'm dad. I'm the law. I'm the nurse. I'm the teacher. I'm the driver. I'm the cook. I'm the freaking Atlas of the family.

I'm waiting for my back to break.

Carter knows. He keeps the world turning and helps me carry it on my shoulders.

I take out my homework, turn on the TV, and try to finish what little I can get done in twenty minutes. Time flies and soon enough Chloe comes bouncing into the house, followed by Abram.

Chloe's happy and hopeful and ignorant.

I love her guts.

Abram's rowdy and dirty and reckless.

I love his guts too.

"Hey Sophie! Can I have a snack?" Chloe smiles at me with her cute face.

I hug her and take her little backpack.

"Of course munchkin." I open her backpack and pull out her spelling words. "Try to spell these out loud while I get some yummies, okay?"

She begins spelling out her first grade words as I cut up a banana that's more brown than yellow.

Michael comes in. We go to the same school, but he has a late class because his grades weren't exactly stellar last year and now he's making up for it.

"Hey," I say.

He mumbles, "hey," back at me. He's way too cool to like his big sister.

I love his guts anyway.

"Have a seat. Pull out your homework." I figured out a year ago the only way to get everyone to do their homework is to make them sit down right after school while they eat something.

The bitter protests the boys give me are expected. I kiss the top of Abram's head and squeeze Michael's shoulder. They hate it when I do that.

But really they don't. They need it.

I grab a couple of apples on the verge of going bad and start cutting them up as well. I don't need a snack. I eat as much as possible at school.

The Littles bicker playfully at the kitchen table as I distribute the meager apple slices. The table wobbles, reminding me to wedge something beneath the uneven legs when I get a chance.

I go to the sink to rinse off the apple knife and glance out my kitchen window into Carter's kitchen. His mom is staggering by the sink and Carter is trying to steady her with his gentle hands.

My heart breaks.

I look at the clock. It's 4:00pm.

I've got five hours until everyone's in bed (or at least in their room for the night). Five hours until I have a minute to think. Five hours until I can connect with the only person who really knows me.

Carter.

CARTER

My mom's not really alive anymore. She's more like a walking, talking, stumbling, slurring ghost.

I'm not mad at her though.

She's sober sometimes; she's crazy all the time.

The pills don't help.

The doctors say she's mentally ill, suffering from extreme hallucinations and paranoia, and the social workers say she should be admitted to a mental care facility. I'm told it's only a matter of time before the state insists on taking her away, but she's the only parent I have left so I'm not ready to let her go. Instead I keep her here and make sure she takes her pills.

But the pills don't help.

It's not her fault though; the craziness, the alcohol. The man who is my father beat the crap out of her for twenty years. His repeated blows to her head damaged her brain and now she self-medicates.

With liquor.

The alcohol numbs the past. And the present. I get it.

I hate it, but I get it.

The man who is my father beat the crap out of me for years too. But I don't think about those years.

"Can't you see them, Carter? They're tiny glass bugs digging into my skin with their claws. Get them off! They're eating me!"

My mom's crazy enough without the alcohol. With the booze, though, she's like gasoline and fire. I look at the empty bottle of Jack by the sink and wonder where she got it. She probably bought it on one of her "good" days and hid it in the house.

I sigh and try to reassure her. "Mom, there are no bugs. You're fine." I say this with sensitivity. I don't talk down to her or belittle her—ever. The man who is my father did enough of that.

"But Carter, I see them! Can you not see them? They're black with green eyes." She's desperately scratching at her skin now.

I sigh and try to take her drunken body into my arms. If I can get her to the couch and turn on some trashy talk show, she'll calm down.

"Don't touch me! They'll get you!" she screams.

I stand very still and play the game. "I promise I won't touch you. What can I do to help? Some bug spray, maybe?"

I want to scream.

Her eyes light up and my chest hurts. "Yes! Oh, Carter, you're amazing. Yes! Bug spray!"

"Okay, stay right here. I'll go get some." I walk down the hall to the closet where we used to keep cleaning agents, chemicals, bleach and, well, bug spray.

A few years ago I got smart and replaced the contents of each bottle with plain water.

I did this after my mom almost died of chemical poisoning because she drank a bottle of kitchen cleaner "to help with the digestion of the gnomes".

I was so afraid she was going to die. After we got home from the hospital, I threw up in the back yard and went into the house to switch out all the cleaners. The real stuff is in my room, locked in a file cabinet.

I grab the fake bug spray and return to the kitchen. My mom's got a knife in her hand, trying to scrape the invisible bugs from her arms.

"Mom, don't!" I freak out, of course.

She looks at me and I try to compose myself. "The, uh, bugs like the steel, mom. You've got to use bug spray." I raise the spray bottle filled with water and pray she believes me.

She nods. "Oh, you're so right. Thank you." She puts down the knife and I exhale.

"Okay, mom. Stand still."

She freezes and I spray her down with misty water, disposing of the nonexistent bugs. She closes her eyes and covers her mouth and nose.

I'm winning her game, but I feel defeated.

She's now damp all over and smiling at me like a little kid at Disneyland. "Thanks sweetie. You're the best son a mama could ever hope for."

I feel like crap.

I smile and lead her into the living room. A talk show is already playing on the TV so I sit her on the sofa and promise to bring her some food. The sofa is orange and brown, torn at almost every seem, and smells like baby powder.

When I was four I dumped an entire bottle of baby powder on the couch because it looked like snow and clouds. My poor mom tried to scrub the powder out for days without success.

So the couch smells like me, when I was four.

And for whatever reason that makes me sad.

I look at my mother, with her messy dark hair and cloudy eyes, and try to see the woman she used to be. I watch her closely, as if at any moment she'll magically awake from this nightmare of a disease and be back to the normal mom she was when I was young.

Nothing changes, though. She's engrossed in her talk show and oblivious to my presence.

I sigh and head back to the kitchen where I brace myself against the stained and cracked countertop. For a moment I close my eyes, listening to the booing audience from the talk show in the other room. My mother starts to boo along with them in excitement. I open my eyes and stare at the kitchen floor.

Once upon a time, she read me books and tied my shoes and played Monopoly with me. Once upon a time, was a beautiful woman with a healthy mind and a loving touch.

That woman is now gone and living in her body is a tortured soul who's been broken.

I hate the monster who broke her.

I look down at the nasty scar that stretches from the back of my neck to my elbow.

The monster broke me too, but I healed. For the most part.

I look out the kitchen window and see Sophie sitting at her table with the kids. The table wobbles as she points to something in front of Abram and nods. There's a plate with some brown fruit on the table.

My chest hurts again.

Chloe spills her cup and water goes everywhere. Sophie starts grabbing homework and papers off the table while the boys are laughing. She throws the papers on the counter and grabs a towel.

Chloe is crying while Sophie sops up the flood that is now on both the table and the floor while Abram and Michael are running though the puddle and sliding across the tile like it's a slip-n-slide.

Sophie takes Chloe into her arms and soothes her with words. The little girl stops crying and smiles up at her big sister. Eventually, Chloe bounces off her lap and scurries away, and Sophie points at the boys and scolds them, swinging her finger toward the other room. The boys follow her orders and leave with their heads down, but they're still smirking.

Alone in the kitchen, Sophie bends to her knees and starts wiping the kitchen floor.

I watch her silently in admiration.

I look at the clock. Just a few more hours.

"Carter, baby. Come in here! I think there's an alligator behind the TV!" My mom's voice is filled with genuine panic.

I stretch my neck and start walking to the living room.

Just a few more hours until I can relax.

SOPHIE

"Abram, if you're going to pee like an animal, then pee in the backyard," I yell down the hallway.

There's pee all over the toilet seat. I clean it up so Chloe can use it. "Go potty and then brush your teeth for me, ok?"

"Okey-dokey," Chloe says.

I close the bathroom door behind me as I leave and hear her start to sing. She always sings when she pees. I love her guts.

I poke my head in Abram's room. "Lights out."

He grumbles and shuts off his lamp. Aside from the peeing-on-the-toilet thing, Abram's a pretty easy twelve-year-old boy. For this, I'm grateful.

Michael walks past me and doesn't make eye contact. He thinks he's the man of the house. And really, he is. But he's also fourteen.

"You too," I say, but not as bossy.

He swings his head to look at me. "Bedtime for a teenager is lame."

I nod because I get it. "Then do whatever you want, but just stay in your room so the kids have some sense of bedtime."

He's mad. "Whatever."

I don't back down or give in. I can't. He still needs me.

After I tuck Chloe in bed, I walk down the hall to the kitchen and start cleaning up the mess from dinner.

We had spaghetti, but we didn't have sauce.

I need to go to the store sometime soon. I need to buy groceries. I need to get the Littles some clothes that fit.

I need to call my mom.

I sit in front of the TV, tuck my hair behind my ear, and work on my homework.

Teachers say you shouldn't watch TV while you do homework, but there's just something about a cheap reality TV show that makes me feel smart.

When I'm trying to solve a difficult math problem or string together an essay for English I can always take a break, watch some realty TV, and think to myself, *well, at least I'm not that drunk girl getting a platypus tattooed on her neck.* Reality TV never fails to boost my ego enough for me to finish my homework on time and vow never to drink myself into a questionable tattoo choice.

Weird how that works out.

I'm a good student, though. I can't afford to mess up at school. I hoping I can get a decent job right out of high school so I can move the Littles someplace else. Somewhere we can be independent.

Somewhere prostitution and drugs and weird boyfriends can't get us.

An hour goes by and I make my way out to the front porch. We have a porch swing. It's like something out of a movie. We look perfect. And I guess that's the point.

Everyone pretends.

The swing squeaks as I sit down and the sound calms me.

The chains are rusted and the wooden planks of the seat and back are splintering in some places, but it's the most beautiful piece of furniture we have.

I rock for a minute, listening to the rhythmic creaking of the swing. The night is quiet except for the crickets. Across the street is a yard filled with cinderblocks, auto parts, and weeds crawling across the ground like the claws of a thorny monster.

But if I close my eyes, and focus only on the singing swing and the chirping crickets, I live in paradise.

I breathe in. I breathe out. I open my eyes.

My heart feels lighter because I know Carter will be here soon. He'll come walking over, sit down next to me, and make my day feel good. My time on the porch swing with Carter every night is the only way I get any sleep.

I see him leave his house sneakily. His mom doesn't care if he's out too late, or gone all together. But she's probably passed out on the couch and Carter's careful not to wake her.

He's a good guy.

He's got a plastic bag with him full of stuff. "Hey, Sophie."

I love how he says my name. It's real.

"Hey, yourself." I smile because I can't help myself. He's big and wonderful and he sits down next to me like I'm important.

He hands the bag to me and looks away. "So…how was your day?"

I look in the bag and want to cry.

It's filled with fresh fruit and raw vegetables and crackers and bread and, well, everything he knows we need.

And he knows what we need.

I love him for this.

I'm terribly moved by the bag of groceries, but I don't cry. He doesn't want me to. He probably doesn't even want me to acknowledge his gift.

I answer him. "It was typical. You?"

We don't look at each other. We stare into the night. It's different now, than it was at school. There's no flirting. No teasing. No laughing high school seniors.

This is reality and with it comes a heaviness.

The night is unusually dark; the streetlights scaring away the stars and the trees hiding the moon. But the darkness is peaceful.

He answers me. "Ah, you know. Gnomes and fake bugs. The usual." He sounds fine. He's not.

I nod because there's nothing to say. We sit in silence, the only noise the slow creaking of the porch swing and the crickets.

He's breathing. I'm breathing.

This is my favorite time of day.

It's easy and calm. There are no crying kids, or strung-out moms, or invisible bugs.

I look down at Carter's arm and eye his long scar.

Or violent dads.

He sees me looking at his scar and shifts in his seat. He's not hiding from me, there's no use. But he doesn't like to talk about his dad and the scar reminds him.

I was ten the first time I saw his dad hurt him. I was in my room staring out my window, wishing we were still in the big city, when I heard a faint howl.

I peeked out my window and saw Carter huddled down in his bedroom. My light was off, but his was on. He was hiding, but his dad found him.

He always found him.

Carter's father used only his hands that night. Blow after blow I watched in horror as Carter's small body became more and more limp. I cried at my window, watching long after his dad had left Carter unconscious on his bedroom floor.

I was ten, I didn't know what to do. I watched and watched until Carter came to and slowly rolled over. His face, his hands, his head, all were bloody. He started crying, which made me cry harder.

I was so scared for him. I trembled in my princess nightgown, safely hidden behind my window in the darkness of my room.

The fights got worse as we grew older. Carter's dad started using baseball bats and golf clubs instead of his hands. I got used to seeing bruises on Carter's body and cuts on his skin.

I told my mom once, about the boy next door whose dad hurt him. My mom said we needed to mind our own business or we would get hurt too.

I was a kid. I believed her.

"We graduate soon." Carter's still looking out at the street. His face is beautiful, even with the scars and the shadows of the night.

I nod. "Yeah. They say that's when life starts. You know, after high school." I'm stressed out all of a sudden.

"Life." Carter scoffs. "Whatever that is."

He's down. I hate it when he gets discouraged. He doesn't think he can have a real life because he needs to take care of his mom. It's a problem without a solution.

"Life is what we make it." I say, but my words sound empty.

He scoffs again, but he's not trying to be mean. "Sometimes I just want to get away from it all, you know?"

I nod. "Yeah. Just pick up and leave. Start over." I sigh. "I think about that all the time."

He nods. "Me too."

We sit in silence for a minute, thinking about the freedom we don't have and the future we can't control.

I pause, trying to figure out how to say what I'm feeling. "It's not all bad, you know." I clear my throat. "At least for me." I shift in the swing. "It's not all stressful and unfair. I have you. You make my life…I don't know…better." My words don't sound empty this time.

He turns to me and cocks his head to the side. He studies me and I don't look away.

I wait.

"Sophie," he says my name again and I'm flying. "You make my life way better than…better."

I know this. I feel it. And I'm grateful for it.

The streetlights turn off and, usually, that's our cue to end our time on the swing, but neither of us moves to leave.

We don't usually touch. We're just friends or whatever. But tonight I decide to do something unusual. I know, even before I move, that I might scare him back into his house. But I don't care.

I reach over and put my hand on his.

Not seductively.

Without expectations.

He turns his hand over to grasp mine.

And we sit, silent and connected at the hand, for long minutes, staring at the dark street.

I'm happy.

CARTER

I'm not sure what to do with Sophie. What to say or how to act. I know she cares about me and that's more than I deserve. So I hold her hand.

If that's what she'll share with me, then I'll take it. She is incredible and I'm lucky to have her in my life. Her hand is cold and small, and fits perfectly in mine. I look down at our hands for a moment.

I know I should go back home and let her get some sleep. I will.

I'm stalling though, because I'm too tired to face the picture of my mom out cold and drooling on the couch. But also because I'm so warm and content on the swing with Sophie. She smells like apples and makes me forget about the junk in my life.

"It gets better, it has to." Sophie's talking about life in general. I envy her positivity and wish I could think the way she does.

"It will, Sophie. You will have a wonderful life." I mean it. She's amazing and will find a way to make her life beautiful.

She looks at me and this time I look back at her. She's so pretty it breaks my heart. Her nose is small and round and her eyelashes are long and dark, feathering against her little girl face. I softly squeeze her cool hand and feel her fingers against my skin.

Touching her makes me realize just how very small she is.

When I watch her throughout the day she seems so...strong. So capable and independent. Sometimes I forget she's just a girl.

Just a girl with tiny hands and big responsibilities.

I look at her closely and my chest hurts. How could a mother abandon this girl?

The man who is my father told me what Sophie's mom was when I was eleven, but I didn't understand what that meant back then.

The reality of Sophie's situation didn't kick in until I was thirteen. The man who is my father had just beat the crap out of me with a two-by-four and I was trying not to cry in my room when I heard Sophie scream.

Looking out my window I saw a big, unfamiliar man standing in Sophie's room, looking like King

Kong while her mom flittered about in front of him trying to shield Sophie.

I noticed Sophie's window was open so I cracked mine to eavesdrop.

"I already paid you! Now move and I'll give you double for the girl." King Kong's voice was booming and full of spit.

"Back off! You got what you came for so leave." Sophie's mom's voice was shaking.

"I'll leave when I please. Now move!" King Kong took a step toward Sophie, who shrieked in response.

I was ready to jump out of my window and run over to Sophie's. I didn't know how I was going to protect her, but I was going to try.

"Get out of my house or I'll call Pete and have the boys maim you!" Sophie's mom looked like an ant compared to the giant man.

Sophie was crying.

I was terrified.

King Kong said nasty things and lunged for Sophie, grabbing her by the hair. Sophie's mom disappeared and returned with a gun, aimed and ready to shoot, so King Kong dropped Sophie and stormed out.

Sophie's mom said sorry, or some other insufficient nonsense, and left the room too. I watched Sophie stay tucked into her bed, with three blankets over her head, and shake for hours.

That was the night I decided Sophie needed protecting. And if I couldn't protect my mom, then I was going to protect the girl next door.

Sophie's voice brings me back to the swing. "We will both have wonderful lives, Carter."

I nod because she wants me to and because I want to believe her. I wish I had money or power so I could make her dreams come true and take away all the bad things.

I don't.

I can't.

I squeeze her hand because I have nothing more to offer.

"Tomorrow morning, then?" she says, and my heart jumps.

I've been going over to Sophie's house every morning before school for a year. Knowing I get to see her first thing in the morning is how I sleep at night.

"Of course," I say, because I wouldn't miss it for the world.

She knows it too.

She winks at me and we pull our hands apart.

It feels wrong, not touching her. Like a piece of me just died or something. But I smile back and make my way off the porch.

"Carter?" she says, and I know what's coming. My heart climbs to the top of my chest in anticipation.

"Sweet dreams," she says casually, like she's done since we were thirteen.

It's impossible. It's cliché. And people say things like that all the time. But those two words used to get me through some bloody nights.

I smile and shove my hands in my pockets. "You too."

I turn and cross the short distance back to my front door.

The doorframe is uneven, making the warped wood of the door stick. I mindlessly yank on the door, releasing it from the splintered frame and evoking a groan from the hinges.

I glance back across the muddy grass, crumbled rock, and cracked concrete that separate us to watch Sophie enter her house quietly.

I will have sweet dreams.

Or at least I won't have nightmares.

SOPHIE

I'm packing lunches and checking homework and making breakfast all at the same time. The TV's on, the radio's on, the frying pan's sizzling, the coffee maker's beeping, and the boys are yelling at each other about a baseball hat.

Total chaos.

This is my every morning.

We're late, I'm stressed, and the eggs are burnt.

Carter walks in with something in his hand. He doesn't have to knock or anything. He's family to me and I like that he walks in.

I calm down immediately.

"Morning." I sound cheerful.

"Morning." He smiles and makes his way to the boys. The baseball hat issue is solved almost immediately and I tell myself to thank Carter for that later.

He's by my side then, teasing me about the eggs and asking me how he can help.

This is *our* every morning.

"Can you grab the kid's lunches and pack them?"

I don't look at Carter. I don't need to. He's good at this. At helping me. At being there.

I pour him a cup of coffee. The Littles and I don't drink coffee, but I make it every morning.

For Carter.

I hand him the mug.

"Thanks." He says, but he looks at me longer than usual.

He loves coffee. It makes him happy or something. He no longer has a coffee maker at his house because his mom kept burning herself and breaking the pot and putting the coffee maker in time out.

So I make him coffee every morning. It makes me feel useful. And happy.

Carter sets down his mug and eyes the kitchen table. He kneels on the floor and starts to wedge the 'something' in his hands under the table legs. I stare with my mouth open as he finishes and stands back up.

The table no longer wobbles.

He busies himself with the lunches as if nothing happened. I stare at the table for a moment, touched by his thoughtfulness.

"Thank you," I say, and mean it from the bottom of my heart.

He shrugs, finishes the lunches and shoves his hands in his pockets.

I love his guts.

I really do.

"Carter, Carter!" Chloe cries with a big smile as she bounces into the kitchen. Carter is her favorite person in the whole wide world. She's informed me that she's going to marry him when she grows up.

He tugs on her pigtails (the ones I spent twenty minutes brushing into place) and kisses the top of her head.

"Morning sunshine." He always calls her sunshine. When she was in kindergarten, she told her teacher that her name was Sunshine.

I make sure everyone eats breakfast and is dressed before ushering everyone out the front door. Then we're off. Everyone heads for school.

Chloe and Abram catch their bus. Michael jogs ahead of me so he's not seen with me when we get to school. And Carter goes back to his house to wake up his mom and make sure she's taken her medicine and whatnot.

Carter's first class of the day starts later than mine.

I go to school all day. I don't see Carter. It's normal.

I'm at lunch, planning on being late for English again when Whitney Morris bombards my personal space and nearly gags me with the scent of her perfume.

"Sophie! I need your help."

No she doesn't.

"Have you talked to Carter, lately?"

"No," I lie as I tuck my hair behind my ear.

Her face falls and I don't feel bad for her.

Whitney sighs dramatically. "It's been five weeks. *Five weeks.* Is Carter seeing someone else?"

Here's the thing about Whitney: I don't like her.

Whitney Morris is popular for all the wrong reasons and happens to be mildly attractive, so people overlook the fact that she's obnoxious.

Not me, though.

Sophomore year, Whitney sat behind me in History and *literally* talked about her pet mouse (that's right, she has a pet mouse—named Minnie) everyday.

Everyday.

Minnie sleeps on a silk pillow. Minnie eats only organic cheese. Minnie gets her nails done once a week.

By the end of sophomore year I was having nightmares about a mouse princess who made me give her pedicures and feed her cheese wedges.

Minnie the mouse haunted my dreams. And completely ruined Disneyland for me.

So Whitney isn't my favorite person. But here she is now, sitting next to me at my lunch table, wanting to talk about her relationship with Carter. And I'd rather sit through a seven-hour description of Minnie Mouse's bowel movements.

Whitney sighs again. "Come on, Sophie. Is there someone else?"

Whitney's in love with Carter and thinks that because they messed around one time they're meant to be together. Basically, she's a slut who needs nonstop attention from guys. I don't say this to be mean, I say this because there are no alternatives.

She knows nothing about Carter.

She's never seen him scared, or watched him take a punch for his mom, or helped him empty all the bottles of alcohol from his house.

She knows nothing.

But she shared her body with him and that makes me hate her.

I don't care how shallow I sound.

I shrug. "How would I know?"

People have no idea that Carter and I are close. We like it that way. It's simple.

Usually.

Whitney rolls her perfect eyes. *"Hello?* You live next door to him. Have you seen anyone go over there?"

I think about it. *The police, the paramedics, the social workers....*

"Nope."

"Ugh!" Whitney's insecure about this, which thrills me.

I don't ever want to see a girl trot into Carter's house like she belongs there. I'm pretty sure I would follow her in and punch her.

"What's the big deal, anyway? Move on." I try to focus on my food. It's important I eat a lot now, otherwise I'll be starving at dinner.

"Move *on*? You don't just *move on* from Carter Jax. He's amazing."

For some reason, I'm feeling incredibly feisty. "Really? How so?"

There's nothing she can tell me that I don't already know.

"Well, for starters, he's an amazing kisser."

Except that.

I might just punch her right now.

"And also, he's got an incredible body."

This I know. I've seen him walking around his house in only a pair of board shorts.

I'm annoyed that her first two examples of how "amazing" Carter is involve his body.

"And he's brave, you know?"

This, from Whitney, surprises me.

I know he's brave. He's the bravest person I've ever met.

I've seen him stand up to a monster of a father and battle a hellish illness with his mother.

I've watched him confront bullies at school for Michael and kill spiders with his bare hands for me.

"I mean," Whitney's voice sounds like nails on a chalkboard to me, "he got in, like, this totally crazy car accident a few years ago and almost died. But he managed to walk himself to a phone and call 911 for help. That's how he got that huge scar on his arm."

Whitney's nodding at me with big, sad eyes and I want to scream. She knows nothing.

I watched that scar get placed on his body.

It wasn't from a car accident, it was from his father.

It happened the August before our junior year of high school. I was doing dishes in the kitchen when I saw Carter's dad swing a baseball bat at his mom.

Carter had been working out that summer and had grown large and strong. He stepped in and grabbed—yes *grabbed*—the baseball bat mid-swing. I immediately ran outside toward his house.

I didn't know what I was going to do but I certainly wasn't going to just wash dishes while Carter got bloodied up by his dad.

I reached his house, all the while looking in the kitchen window, and I saw his dad come at him with a butcher knife.

I remember feeling numb all over. I was suffocating and stopped running. I watched in frozen silence as Carter's body was slashed open and blood flew around the kitchen.

I thought he was dead.

Then I would be dead, too.

But Carter stood up tall, grabbed his father (who was smaller in comparison at that point) and threw him against the wall. Carter punched him over and over again with his bloody hands.

Carter was screaming and crying, his fury raining down in the form of fists and kicks and sweat and blood.

I stood in their yard as Carter heaved his father's pummeled body out onto the front porch. His dad was unconscious, but not dead.

When Carter saw me he immediately began apologizing and stuttering and trying to wipe off the blood that kept pouring out of him.

I did the only thing I could think of. I ran over to him, wrapped my arms around him and told him he was brave and right and wonderful. I think we both cried while his bloody arm stained my clothes and scared the crap out of me.

That's how he got his scar.

I drove Carter to the hospital that night.

I sat next to him while he got stitches.

I made him dinner for the next two weeks because his arm was useless and his mom had lost her mind.

I was there.

Not Whitney.

Carter's dad never came back after that night.

I look at Whitney and fake my response. "Wow, really? Yeah, that's brave." I bite my cheek so I don't strangle her.

"I really felt like we connected, you know? Like we totally clicked. So I don't understand why he's not calling me back."

They so did not totally click.

"Did he say he'd call you back?" I ask, looking innocent.

I know the answer. Because, after all, I know *him*.

"Well, no. He said he doesn't do relationships and that his life is too complicated for anything serious so I shouldn't waste my time with him."

He always warns them.

"Was that before or after you messed around with him?"

Suck it, Whitney Morris.

She thinks about it. "Well…I guess he said that before…."

"Then there's your answer," I snap. She doesn't get my pity.

"Well *excuse* me. I didn't know dating Evan Walters made you Queen of Relationships." She's trying to be snotty. It's not going to work.

I shrug and she gets up and leaves with a huff.

I used to date a guy named Evan Walters. Evan is the guy every girl at school wants to date. He's hot, he's wealthy, he's a football player. He's every girl's dream.

Except mine.

Evan isn't a bad guy. He's actually pretty nice and not too stuck up. And I really did like him quite a bit. So much so, that I felt like I had to pretend I had a perfect home life just to maintain our relationship.

Because Evan doesn't understand real life and I could never trust someone like him with the truth about me.

So we broke up. I wasn't sad afterwards. I probably should have been, but I wasn't. Unfortunately, now I have this label slapped on my back that reads "Evan's Ex-Girlfriend" and it's extremely inconvenient.

Whatever.

I hate Whitney Morris and I wish Evan Walters would go to a different school.

I close my eyes and try to push Whitney and Evan away from my thoughts.

I'm graduating in two weeks. After that, nothing will matter.

Except me.

And the Littles.

And Carter.

CARTER

In my last class of the day, TJ is trying to convince me go to some kegger. I don't drink, but TJ doesn't know that. He doesn't know anything really.

"I think that kid Evan is bringing the beer. You know him, right? I think he was messing around with your neighbor for a while."

Well, TJ knows *that*.

I hate that TJ knows that.

And I hate Evan Walters.

And I hate that I hate these things. It means I care—which I do. But I wish I didn't care so much. It's unhealthy.

When I first heard Sophie was with Evan, I didn't sleep for three nights. Three *freaking* nights. That's unhealthy.

But I couldn't help myself. The idea of Sophie and Evan together pricked at my mind until I was a crazed insomniac.

Sophie's not just any girl so she shouldn't be with just any guy.

She should be...I don't know...just *not* dating Evan Walters.

"—so hot. Have you ever seen her naked, man? Like from your window?"

I realize TJ's talking to me again and I'm annoyed. "Who?"

TJ stares at me. "Sophie Hartman, dude. Isn't she a total hottie?"

I blink a few times. "Yeah, Sophie's gorgeous. No, I've never seen her naked." But now I'm thinking about it.

Freaking TJ.

"I hear her mom's kinda easy. Maybe the girl is too." TJ's raising his eyebrows like a pig.

When Sophie and I were Freshmen, her mom would only disappear for a few days at a time. I know because I'd watch their house closely, waiting for her mom to come home so I could relax.

Although, even when she was home I never relaxed.

The first time her mom had been gone for a whole week, I remember taking the trash out one night and seeing Sophie at her kitchen table, crying.

I don't know why I did it, but I walked over to her front door and let myself in. I knew if I knocked she would have just ignored me.

I walked into the kitchen to find her looking at me, not surprised to see me. I sat down at the table next to her.

"It'll be okay." I didn't have anything better to say.

After a while I put my arm around her and squeezed her shoulder. She tucked her wet face into my arm and said, "Thank you."

That was the first time in my life I'd ever felt important.

"Sophie's not like that," I say absently.

"How would you know?" TJ looks at me closely.

I forget, momentarily, that Sophie and I aren't supposed to know one another at school.

"I don't. I'm just guessing." I shrug and stretch my neck, like Sophie's *not* the best part of my every day.

"That's not what Evan said."

TJ's an infant.

My blood is boiling and I'm trying to reason with myself. I'm not her boyfriend or anything. I'm not anyone who has any right to feel possessive about Sophie.

But I do.

I can't stop myself. I don't want to stop.

She's tough and incredible and beautiful...and she's a better person than anyone I know.

Screw Evan Walters.

"Evan sucks." I shouldn't have said that, but I don't feel bad. I stretch my neck again as TJ laughs at me.

"Whoa, man. You got a thing for this girl or what?" He seems confused.

I don't care.

The bell rings, freeing me from answering his question. I jet out of school and start heading home.

Sophie's already in front of me, looking pretty and gentle. She doesn't drop any notes today and for some reason I think she's mad at me.

SOPHIE

I spent all afternoon trying to shake off my jealousy. Turns out you can't shake jealousy off. You've got to pet it and lie to it and soothe it until it settles comfortably in the back of your mind.

And then wait until another one of Carter's love interests comes along and wakes it up. Ugh.

I've been banging pots and pans tonight while making dinner. The Littles know something's up, but I'm talking like I'm fine.

I lie, just like any other parent.

I look at our food while we're eating dinner and I'm thankful Carter was so generous to us. This softens my heart enough to think about him without getting all crazy-ex-girlfriend.

My brain's not done stressing, though.

We still need money. Rent is behind. Chloe needs new shoes. And I if I don't pay the electric bill soon we'll be living in darkness..

Bedtime is a breeze for some reason. I think the Littles are afraid to tick me off. So everyone's either asleep or quiet in their room by 8:30pm.

I wander out to the swing early because I need...something.

I'm not sure what it is, but I know sitting on the swing for a minute will help me figure it out. Carter's already there, sitting on the porch steps, playing with a stick.

My heart fills up.

That's what I needed. Carter.

"Hey, Sophie," he says, and we make our way over to the swing.

"Hey." I smile as we sit down next to each other.

We're silent, letting the peace we bring one another fill the cracks in our lives.

I clear my throat. I'm nervous.

Why am I nervous?

I say, "Remember when we were thirteen and fourteen and we would sneak out at night and meet at the Big Oak?"

The Big Oak is this huge tree between our houses. It's in the back so our parents couldn't see us from the house. We thought we were so clever and sly.

He smiles. "Yep. Picnics in the dark."

I nod slowly and tuck my hair behind my ear. "Picnics in the dark." I shift on the swing, making it creak. "I would bring a blanket and you would bring leftovers and we'd pretend our lives weren't crappy."

I think back to those nights.

We would lie on our backs and stare up at the few stars we saw peeking between the dense branches of the tree. We would talk and laugh and sigh. It was wonderful.

I hear Carter breathing and it's soothing.

He says, "Yeah, we'd talk about our futures and how we were going to run away from home and go get famous in Hollywood."

I smile. "Ah, yes. Hollywood. I forgot about that."

It's funny how, when you're little, you really *do* believe anything is possible.

Carter turns and smiles. It's the kind of smile I haven't seen in a long time. It's the smile of a little boy without the stress of a man.

He says, "Remember when we first got our drivers' licenses? We would drive out to the old mining caves on Friday nights and smoke cigarettes and whine about our parents?"

I nod and smile. The day we turned sixteen was fun. We have the same birthday, May 12th. We don't smoke, but when we were sixteen, we thought we were cool and stole cigarettes from my mom.

"It was beautiful out there…all those stars," I say.

The first time we went to the caves was the first time I really saw how starry the night sky was without the light pollution of the city.

Those were good times. It was just the two of us. Just friends. Just trying to survive.

That was just a few months before Carter beat his dad up. I remember because that whole summer Carter had a nasty black bruise on his back from being hit repeatedly with a wrench.

"Yeah," he says. "The sky was awesome out there."

We're looking at each other and it's different than usual. Not weird, but not the same. There's something in the silence. I can feel it.

We don't break our gaze

"So how was your day?" I ask, because I have no other words.

"Uneventful. Paranoid mom yelling at the TV all day. No issues." He looks old when he says this and I wish I could hug him. "Yours?"

I look out at the street and think about what happened at lunch today, "Crappy." That's all I say.

My day wasn't that bad, but the Whitney thing along with the money stress is taking its toll.

We sit for a minute and I'm falling into our comfortable silence when Carter reaches over and gently wraps his fingers around my hand.

My day just went from crappy to great.

CARTER

Sophie's hand feels good in mine. She doesn't pull away and that's more than I deserve.

We sit for a while, holding hands, rocking on the swing like an old married couple. It doesn't bother me. It makes me happy.

"Whitney's asking about you again." She says this softly, but I hear something else behind her words. I don't know what it is.

I sigh. "Sorry, that's probably annoying. I'll ask her to leave you alone."

I feel guilty all of a sudden.

I shouldn't feel guilty. I didn't do anything wrong. Did I?

Sophie and I have talked about Whitney before. This shouldn't be as heavy as it feels.

Should it?

"No, no. Don't say anything to her. It's fine." Sophie sighs. "Besides, if you call her, even to tell her to back off, she'll just think you're interested."

That *something* was there again in Sophie's voice. What was it?

"I'm a jerk." I lean back into the swing.

Sophie ponders. "No, you're honest. You told her how you are about relationships. It's her fault for thinking she could change you."

I sit up.

Hurt. That's what I hear in Sophie's voice.

She's…something. Mad? Offended? Sad?

Jealous?

I know it's sick, but my heart skips a beat at the thought of Sophie being jealous.

I don't know what to say, so I say the stupidest thing that could come out of my mouth. "Talk to Evan lately?"

Her hand tenses in mine and I immediately regret asking. I suck.

When I first found out Sophie and Evan were together—during my crazed insomniac phase—I marched over to her house, walked right in, and proceeded to tell her all the reasons why she shouldn't *be* with a guy like Evan.

None of the reasons included me. Because I'm a chicken.

I made her cry that night. Worst night of my life.

She forgave me because she's a better person than I am, but I'm an idiot for bringing Evan up again.

"*No*," she says through her teeth. "Trying to keep tabs on my love life?" There's so much venom in her voice I almost drop her hand.

But I can't, because I'm connected to her and she gives my life purpose.

We're both stare at the road.

"No," I say.

"Good, because that would be highly hypocritical."

She's mad. About more than just the Evan thing.

"Are you upset about Whitney?"

Why did I just say that? It's like I *want* to pick a fight or something.

She pulls her hand out of mine and a piece of me dies. She turns to face me, mouth open, but not saying anything.

Then I realize why I said that.

Because I knew I was right.

I knew Sophie was jealous and I wanted to goad her.

I'm a sick, twisted person.

Sophie composes herself then opens her mouth again. "Whitney? No, Carter, I'm not upset about *Whitney*. Although I don't know what you saw in her.

She's shallow and obnoxious and...just *wrong* for you."

"Wrong for me?"

She nods. "All wrong. All of your little flirty fan club members are. And you have the *audacity* to judge *me* for dating one guy—*one freaking guy*—who is, according to you, Your Majesty, all wrong for me."

She's right, but I'm too mad to care. "He was wrong for you!"

"So?"

"So? You've got *stuff* in your life that can mess with your head. And being with some dumb jock is only going to make it worse!"

"So what, then? My mommy's a hooker so I've got to be a nun to compensate?"

She's so mad, I'm scared she's going to cry.

But I don't stop, because I'm stupid.

"Of course not. I just think you need someone who gets it, you know?" I don't know what I'm saying but my chest hurts.

"No, I don't know, because all I hear you saying is that I need to be with someone who 'gets it' but you can be with whoever you want!"

I try to calm down and lower my voice. "But the difference is that you were *into* Evan. You cared about him. I'm not like that with Whitney—or any of those other girls." I swallow and stretch my neck.

It feels sticky outside all of the sudden.

"Why aren't you into those girls?" Sophie asks.

I have no idea. I really don't know. I'm trying to think of some excuse I can spew at her but she sees through me. Of course.

There's a sharpness to her voice now. "Because if you let them get to know you then you'll be completely exposed? Vulnerable?"

I think about it for a long minute, turn back to look at her and answer honestly. "Yes."

"Well, too bad, Carter! That's what life's about. There is no meaning in life unless you're sharing it, *really sharing it*, with other people. So you can hide your past, and lie about your scars, and pretend all you want. But pretending you're someone else with those other girls will never, never take away the pain!"

Her voice doesn't waiver and I'm stunned. She just called me out. And of course, she's right.

"I know." My voice is quiet.

We stop looking at each other and stare back out at the street.

I exhale.

She exhales.

Minutes pass.

"The same goes for you too, though," I say gently.

We both lean back in the swing and slowly rock.

"I know," she says.

She wiggles her hand back into mine without a word and it's the best thing I've ever felt.

We're good again.

SOPHIE

It's Saturday and we can't go much longer without money. So after three hours of prepping myself for an emotional train wreck, I call my mom. Or rather, I call Pete the pimp.

"Your ma's not with me anymore."

At first I think this means she's dead.

"She moved on. Wanted to go independent or somethin' like that." Pete sounds like he smells bad. "She broke my heart, your mama."

He's a pimp so I don't care. "Do you know where I can reach her?"

"No, darling. Not unless you'd be willing to sub in while she's gone." His voice is dripping with nasty.

"Listen, Pete. Give me her number and I'll try to talk her into coming back to you. Sound good?"

He doesn't buy it, but he caves anyway. "I don't have a number. But I hear she's dancing at Low Lou's these days."

Dancing, huh? Well, I guess mama's moving up in the world.

"Thanks," I say and hang up on his smarmy face.

My palms are sweating and my stomach is churning. I do not—cannot—go see my mother. It will tear my heart to look at her in person, see the "dancer" she is and the mother she is no longer.

I need back up.

"Michael!" I holler.

He comes slinking down the hallway, half-interested.

"Hey, I've got to go get mom's paycheck downtown. Can you watch the kids tonight?" It's not really a question; it's more like an order. Michael knows it.

"Her paycheck? You mean you've got to go get the cash she's been collecting with her body?"

Crap, he knows.

I shouldn't be surprised.

"Yeah," I say. "She's dancing at Low Lou's now."

"Classy."

I nod, take a deep breath, and tuck my hair behind my ear. "Anyway, we need the money, so I've got to go. Are you good here?"

"Yeah, but you should take someone with you. I hear bad stuff about that area. And you're, you know, a girl."

It's the most caring thing Michael's ever said to me.

I give him a small smile. "Yeah, I'm going to ask Carter to go with me."

I grab my stuff and head out the front door, but turn around at the last second. "Hey, Michael?"

He looks at me.

"Are you okay with…you know?" I shift my weight.

"With mom being a hooker? No. Of course not. But I don't really think of her as my mother, you know?" He shuffles his feet and looks around. "I've got you. We've got you. We're good as our own little family or whatever."

My heart is warm and singing.

"I love you," I say, because I love his guts and he doesn't hear it enough.

"Ick. Just go," he says, but he's smiling. He loves me too.

With that, I leave and knock on Carter's door.

He answers in only a pair of board shorts and for whatever reason I start blushing.

He's so muscular and…big. His long scar is fading. His other scars, the smaller ones that mark up most of his beautiful body, are fading too.

Scars fade. I wonder if pain and hurt fade too.

"Hey, Sophie. What's up?" He smiles.

I pull my eyes away from his lovely body. "I need backup. I've got to go see my mom."

"Nope." He shakes his head. "No way. You are not walking into some prostitution den for cash. I'll rob a bank before I let you do that."

His protectiveness should irk me, but instead it makes me feel safe. It takes me a second to respond.

"She's dancing now, at Low Lou's. I've just got to go down there, grab some cash, and get some contact info from her."

Carter hesitates.

"Please?" I totally cheat and pout my lips and bat my lashes. He can't say no.

He sighs. "All right. Let me get dressed."

He doesn't invite me in because he doesn't have to. It's our understanding. I follow him inside as he disappears down the hallway. I look around his house as I stand awkwardly just outside the living room.

The ceiling is low, making the room feel darker and smaller than it actually is, and the brown carpet is thin and worn.

Around the living room I see familiar patches of drywall touch-ups from the various holes Carter's father put in their walls. His temper didn't always start or end with Carter's body. The house took a beating as well.

I enter the living room, the smell of baby powder and dust greeting me.

Carter's mom is there, on the couch, looking at me like I'm a piece of candy and she's a five-year-old.

"Carter stopped the flood, you know," she says.

I don't know, but I nod because she's a ticking time bomb of crazy.

She continues, "The milk spilled because of those darn rabbits, and it started filling up the whole house. I thought I was gonna drown in milk. But Carter's a smart boy. He opened the back door and drained it all out. Chased away the bunnies, too."

I nod and smile. "That's good to hear. I'm glad you're okay."

Of course there hadn't been any milk flood or rabbits. But Carter goes along with the insanity because he knows it's easier for her.

That's love.

I'd probably try to reason with my mom if she were crazy. I'd argue and yell and fight, until both of us were in tears.

That's why Carter's a better person than I am.

He sees her anguish and bends over backwards to make her world less frightening.

"It's all this mangled hair that makes me blind, you know? I keep trying to cut it all off, but Carter hides the scissors." Carter's mom grabs a hairbrush off the coffee table and tries to brush through her mane.

Her hands are too shaky to be effective. They shake because of the pills. And the alcohol. And the craziness.

I've seen Carter try to brush his mother's hair. He's so careful and patient, but she's always yelling at him and struggling.

"Let me, Mrs. Jax." I slowly walk over to her, expecting her to throw the brush at me and accuse me of eating her daffodils or something. But she doesn't.

She smiles at me sweetly and holds out the brush. I tuck my hair behind my ear and take it from her soft hand.

I remember Mrs. Jax before she was broken. She was sweet. Timid and shy, but sweet. My heart falls, because I know the old Mrs. Jax will never be back.

I gently start brushing her tangled hair. It's pretty and hasn't lost any of its color yet.

"Carter is a good man, Mrs. Jax. He loves you quite a bit." I call Carter a man and it doesn't feel wrong.

"And when Carter loves something, he is fierce about it." I say the words before I realize they're true. I run the brush slowly through the tips of her hair and continue, "He protects it…and cares for it…and devotes himself to it."

All true.

I concentrate on Mrs. Jax's hair as I think through my words. I'm trying to assure her of her son's love. Because I know what it looks like when Carter loves something. I've seen him give his all to his mother. I've seen his love at work.

Her hair softens with each stroke of the brush. "And Carter…he's loyal when he loves. He always shows up and makes everything better. He listens and he's patient…."

My eyes start to water and I swallow.

"He's gentle with what he loves and he'd do anything to protect it…."

I swallow again because I've just realized, for the first time in all these years, that Carter loves *me*.

I go on, because even though his mom might not understand Carter's love, I do. "He's careful with what he loves, and he's scared of losing it."

I keep running the brush slowly through her tendrils, trying to keep my voice from cracking with emotion. "But there are some kinds of love that you can't lose, no matter how hard you try. So there's no need for him to be afraid."

Her hair is smooth now. I run my fingers through it and wish Mrs. Jax's mind was as healthy as her hair. I look down at her and she's fallen asleep.

A tear falls from my face and lands on the brown floor. I hurry to wipe my cheeks before I completely lose it.

I think I've always known that I love Carter. But now I know he loves me too—even if he doesn't know it.

CARTER

I'm silent in the hallway, not because I'm trying to be sneaky, but because I've forgotten how to speak.

I can see Sophie—sweet, beautiful Sophie—trying to dry her face with her tiny hands. I just want to hold her. Like she's a doll or something. I want to hold her, and kiss her, and feed her and dance with her and tuck her in at night.

She brushed my mom's hair.

She's the most amazing girl I've ever known.

I'm quiet because I'm trying to keep myself from shouting something stupid like, "Sophie, I would die for you! Will you please always hold my hand on the swing!"

I'm pathetic.

I clear my throat as I enter the living room and Sophie looks up at me like nothing's wrong. Like she didn't just brush my crazy mom's hair and talk about how great my ability to love is.

My chest hurts.

"Hey," she says, and I play along with her.

"Hey." I look at my sleeping mom and glance at Sophie. "Thank you."

She nods because what else can she say?

Sophie goes to the kitchen and I carry my mom to her room and tuck her into bed. She mumbles something about rodents with spatulas and I ignore it.

When I get back to the kitchen, Sophie is waiting for me. I stop walking and look at her for a long time.

Instead of asking me what's wrong or why I'm staring at her like a weirdo, she just stands still and silently lets me take her in.

She's the most beautiful thing I've ever seen. And not just because she's got a hot body and flawless skin and smells like apples. But because she's in my kitchen.

Without judgment.

Without fear.

She's standing in my house, where she knows me and all my demons, looking at me with nothing but love.

I'm in love with Sophie Hartman and it scares the crap out of me.

"We should go," she says softly.

I nod my head and we leave.

We get in my old truck and drive downtown. We're quiet the whole way there. It's tense in the truck, so we let the silence float.

I want to hold her hand, but it's different now.

I feel like if I touch her hand I won't be able to let go.

Ever.

I'm scared out of my mind.

Miles and miles we drive in silence.

"Are you nervous?" I ask. It's a rhetorical question. Of course she's nervous.

She inhales. "Yeah. I'm mostly freaked out about seeing her in, you know, her *element*."

I nod. I can't imagine what that's like.

"It'll be fine. *You'll* be fine," I say, and I mean it.

The sun is starting to set as we enter downtown. Low Lou's is a shady place at the end of 1st street. I park the truck and we both sit there, not moving, for a few minutes.

Sophie's trying to prepare herself. She's trying not to care.

She's breaking my heart.

"Sophie," I say, and she looks at me with her little girl eyes.

I'm a goner.

I clear my throat. "No matter what happens in there, no matter what you see or feel, I want you to know that you are incredible. You are brave and wise and strong. None of your mother's choices have anything to do with you, okay? You are your own person. And at the end of this day, you will still be Sophie. And I will still be here for you. Always." I pause, because I'm close to saying I love you and completely freaking her out. "Okay?"

A tear falls from her face and I can't help myself. I brush my thumb across her wet cheek and cup her face in my hand. This is the first time I've ever touched her face.

If I die right now, I'll die happy.

She tilts her head into my hand and closes her eyes as she takes a deep breath.

I pull her to my chest and press her against my heart. She doesn't resist. She folds herself into me like she was meant to be there. She's so small and warm and fragile. I wrap my arms around her, never wanting to let go.

Right here, in my old truck, in the middle of seedy downtown, is the best moment of my life.

Because Sophie's safe.

Sophie's in my arms.

And I have no more demons.

I kiss the top of her head because it feels right. I've never kissed her before.

Why haven't I ever kissed her before? Why don't I ever pull her into my arms like this? Why have I never touched her soft face before today?

What have I been waiting for?

A minute passes and she looks up at me, no longer crying. "Okay, I have to do this."

Our moment is over, so I slowly release her hand.

SOPHIE

Touching Carter makes everything better. My heart has cracks and scars and horror stories, but Carter makes me forget about the pain.

I need him.

I love him.

I can't be whole without him.

I reluctantly move farther away from Carter and his familiar ocean scent, and get out of the truck. I walk up to the bouncer standing outside Low Lou's, trying to look like I want to be there, with Carter right behind me.

"ID's," the bouncer growls. He's a bald giant, with a dark goatee and tattoos covering his throat.

At least my mom now works someplace where identification is required. That's got to be a little safer than the open admission policy she had under Pete.

Carter and I show him our ID's. We're legal. Yay.

We enter the strip bar and everything inside me screams *Run away! Run away!* But I don't, of course. I've got children to feed. I've got a family to take care of.

Ugh.

It takes a minute for our eyes to adjust to the darkness. The air is thick with smoke and smells stale. I can make out silhouettes of people in the back corner, but no faces.

Carter takes the lead and I follow him like a puppy. A safe puppy.

He walks up to the bartender and asks if my mom is working tonight.

The bartender is an overweight man who looks like he's in his fifties, but he's probably no older than thirty-five. He's wearing gaudy gold rings on six of his chubby fingers and he has a cigarette in his mouth.

When he finishes smearing the grime from a dirty rag onto the bar, he looks up and gives us a lecture about calling ahead and waiting lists and pricing. Then he tries to sell us on a different stripper named Cotton Candy, all the while keeping his cigarette balanced in the corner of his mouth. A half-dressed woman—who I can only assume is Cotton Candy—walks past the bar and winks at Carter.

I think I might be sick.

"Actually," I respond because I'm losing my patience—and my stomach, "I'm her daughter. I need to see her."

The bartender looks at me suggestively.

Carter shifts so he's more in front of me.

"Thinking of a mommy-daughter act, sweet cheeks? Lou loves those kinda shows. I bet he'd even give ya prime time with a body like that."

He's staring at my chest and I feel exposed, even though my shirt more than covers me.

I hear Carter growl so I quickly say, "No. I need to *talk* to her."

The bartender says, "We don't do none of that family drama in here, ya understand? I'll tell her she's got visitors, but if ya cause a scene, I'll kick you out of here, got it?"

I hate the bartender, but I nod anyway.

Carter's hand is suddenly on the back of my arm and I'm safe again. We don't speak, probably because I'm close to vomiting, but we understand each other. His hand slowly runs downs my arm and finds my hand. He weaves his fingers in between mine and I want to jump into his arms.

The bartender leads us to a darkened doorway and points to the back.

This time I lead the way, with Carter connected to me at the hand. We pass the bartender and enter what looks like a dressing room.

Around us there are naked strippers running around, makeup strewn about vanities, and lingerie littering the floor.

And right smack dab in the middle of the mess is my mom. A tiny sequined vest is squeezing her boobs together. Other than that she's wearing nothing but a thong.

And a wasted grin.

"Sophie, baby! What are you doing here?" She comes over and throws her arms around me. She's hugging me like I'm a long lost girlfriend. Not her tired, hungry little girl.

She smells like smoke and vanilla.

"Hey, mom. I, uh—"

"Ruby! Get over here! Come meet my baby!"

My mom's happy. *Very* happy. Which means the heroine has set in.

Or the meth.

Or the coke.

I let go of Carter's hand so I can rub my sweaty palm on my pants.

"Trophy, I didn't know you had a girl." Ruby appears from around the corner, topless. She takes in Carter and purrs. "Oh, honey, please tell me this isn't your boy, 'cause you *know* I like 'em young!"

I almost spit on Ruby.

Instead I turn to my mother, confused. *"Trophy?"*

"Yeah, baby. That's my stage name. Like it? Now our names rhyme!" She's excited about this. She thinks it's fun.

Ruby leaves our conversation and I'm grateful she took her naked boobs with her.

I look at my mom. Her body is skinny, bruised, and has a very fake tan. I want to pick her up, give her a bath, and wrap her in a muumuu.

"Huh." That's all I say. I hate that my mom has a stage name.

"So darlin', what brings you here? How did you know where to find me?"

She's pleasant. She doesn't realize she switched professions without leaving a forwarding address.

"Pete, mama. He told me I could look here."

She waves me off. "That Pete was a complete loser."

No duh.

"Uh, mama. I came to see you because rent is due, and the kids need some new clothes—"

"Kids? Trophy, you got more rugrats at home?" Ruby is back, but this time with a top on.

"Yeah, Rubes. I got two boys."

I try to hide my disgust at her forgetfulness. "And *Chloe*, mama."

She gasps. "Oh, that's right! I got little Chloe back home!" She giggles like it's hilarious that she forgot about her own child. "How old is little miss Chloe these days? Two? Three, now?"

I hate my mother.

"Six, mama."

"Six! Wow, time flies."

I move back a step and feel Carter's chest behind me. It's comforting. It's the only thing keeping me from screaming.

I continue, "Right, so the kids, *all* the kids, need clothes and rent is due—"

She waves me off again. "Say no more sweetie pie."

She digs around in a knockoff designer purse on the nearest vanity and pulls out a wad of bills. She shoves the money at me and smiles.

"Big money in dancin', darlin'. Mama's been real good this month."

I clutch my stomach, trying to keep my insides from spilling out. I grab the bills and flatten them so they'll fit in my wallet. I notice they're all hundreds.

"Mom, there's like…" I count. "Three thousand dollars here."

"I know, baby!" she squeaks with a smile. I notice her front tooth is cracked. "I told you there's good money here!" She looks me up and down like she's never seen me before. "You know, you would make *big* money here, Sophie. I mean *big money*! Why, you and I together could pull in five grand a night."

She's serious.

"Want me to talk to Lou, sweetie pie?" She's looking at me with genuine excitement and my heart completely severs.

She's no longer my mother.

She is a woman who gave birth to four kids and left three of them in my care. She's how I pay bills. That's all.

I decide I'm getting a good job as soon as I graduate because I will never again take her dirty money.

"Uh no, mama." My voice cracks and I'm close to tears.

"Honey, what's wrong? Are you sick, baby?"

Of course she thinks I'm sick. She's too strung out to realize I'm suffering from a broken heart.

Carter speaks and my heart calms down. "I think we need to go."

"Oh, I'm so rude. Sophie, who's your friend here?" My mom looks at Carter.

"This is Carter." I say. She doesn't recognize him so I prompt, "From next door?"

She raises her eyebrows in surprise. "Oh, Carter! Your daddy used to beat you, right? Terrible thing about your mama losing her mind. How ya holdin' up, deary? No broken bones, I see."

I hate her.

If I stay for another minute I'll strangle her.

"No, Mrs. Hartman. No broken bones," Carter says politely.

I'm pretty sure I'm on the verge of a mental breakdown.

"I've got to go." I don't say bye. I don't call her mama. I just turn around and leave.

I'll never see her again and that liberates me.

It also kills me.

Carter's behind me as we exit the club. He shuffles me into the truck and drives us away, the buildings blurring together as we leave downtown.

It's dark outside.

We've been driving for a long time and I can see stars against the black sky.

I haven't cried yet. I'm too numb to cry.

Carter pulls off onto a dirt road and I know where he's going and love him for it.

Now I do start to cry because he's so great and he knows me so well.

He reaches his hand out and covers mine. He thinks I'm crying because of my mom, but I'm not.

I'm crying because the boy next door loves me, and it's the best thing that's ever happened to me.

CARTER

I can't bring myself to take Sophie back home yet so I'm driving out to the old mining caves.

It's the one place that feels like our own; empty of people and full of the sky.

When we get there, I park in the dirt and lean over, silently kissing the top of Sophie's head.

She's crying and I'm helpless.

I can't take away any of the hard stuff she deals with so I do the next best thing.

I get out, open her door, pull her out, and sit her on the back of the truck.

It's what we used to do.

Before.

We sit on the back of my truck and stare at the stars. We haven't been here for a long time.

There are no cigarettes, this time. Just more brokenness.

But there's something else, too.

Love.

Not the kind you see in the movies or hear about on the radio.

The real kind.

The kind that gets beaten down and bloody, yet perseveres.

The kind that hopes even when hope seems foolish.

The kind that forgives. The kind that believes in healing.

The kind that can sit in silence and feel renewed.

The *real* kind of love.

It's rare and we have it.

Our feet dangle off the edge of the truck as we look out into the darkness. Sophie sighs and leans against me. She smells like apples and tears.

I let her finish crying before I speak. "Sorry about tonight."

She nods. "Me too."

We wrap our hands together and don't speak.

We sit like that for hours. Sophie leaning against me, breathing in softly, and me rubbing my thumb across her hand. It's a good ending to a bad day. It's not a happy ending, but it's good.

Someday, I'll make sure it's happy.

SOPHIE

The Littles are hyper on this Monday morning, excited for the end of school carnival later this week. I'm excited too. Not for the carnival, but for the end of school. I'll be done. I'll be free to make a new life for all of us.

I'm running around, frantically trying to get lunches and backpacks and breakfast done.

Carter couldn't come over this morning. He called to say his mom had an episode and had shattered all of their glasses. He was busy combing the house for overlooked shards that could cut bare feet.

He's a good guy.

I get everyone out the door, grab a mug full of hot coffee, and lock up.

The Littles leave in their general directions as I walk up to Carter's door. I open it and peek inside.

Carter's on his hands and knees, squinting under the dining table. He sighs and I clear my throat.

He looks up, not surprised to see me.

"Morning, Sunshine" I say with a smile. It makes him smile back and I feel victorious.

"Morning," he says.

"I brought you coffee." I take it over to him as he stands up. It's steaming hot. I put it in his favorite mug.

He looks down at the coffee, looks at me, and twitches his mouth.

I think he's going to say something, but he's interrupted by his mother's shrill cry.

"Carter! The aliens are back! I need more glass! I need more glass!"

He looks defeated. "I'll be right back."

I stop him. "No, let me."

He's shaking his head, ready to argue.

So I put on my stubborn face and use my mom voice. "I know the game, Carter. I can do this. You sit down and drink your coffee. Pretend you're a normal guy who reads the newspaper in the morning and actually likes the taste of black coffee." I smile and hurry to the living room.

Mrs. Jax is crouched down in the corner, armed with a plastic vase.

"Hey, Mrs. Jax. Carter said you're having a problem with aliens." I say this sincerely. Mocking her does no good.

"Yes, yes. They're everywhere and they want me!"

I nod and look around purposefully. "Okay, here's what we'll do. I'll tell Carter to get the glass and, in the meantime, I'll brush your hair, okay? Aliens hate hairbrushes, they won't come near you." I smile at her.

She nods and I'm flooded with relief. I find a hairbrush and begin to tame her wild hair.

"The aliens are real, you know," she says.

"I know."

"They've been in my head for years. Telling me lies."

This makes me sad. In a way, I'm sure it's true. "That's awful. Can you tell them to leave you alone?"

Her hair softens in my hands.

"Oh, sure. But they don't listen. They're in there good, you know?"

"I'm so sorry, Mrs. Jax. That must be frustrating."

"It is. I could kick them out, but then where would I be?"

I don't know how to answer this so I say nothing.

Mrs. Jax continues, "I'd be back to the monster, that's where. And I don't ever want to see the monster again."

She's probably talking about some furry, orange thing that sleeps under her bed, but I respond as if she's talking about Carter's dad.

"He was a bad monster," I say, and I want to cry for all the damage the monster did.

"Yes," she says softly, "he was."

"You're a good woman, though, Mrs. Jax. That monster can't get you now."

Her hair is nearly finished.

She sighs and leans her head back into me. "The rabbits would like you."

I nod.

CARTER

I'm staring at the coffee mug like it's a foreign object. Sophie brought me coffee. It's no big deal. But it is.

She loves me.

It's just not the coffee. Or the fact that she's brushing my mom's hair.

It's not just the notes she drops for me on the way home from school. Or the way she waits for me on the swing.

It's all of those things.

And more.

Sophie walks into the kitchen and eyes me curiously. I look dumb because I'm standing there, staring at my coffee cup, not doing anything.

She smiles at me with her pretty face and my heart pumps faster. She knows all about me. And still she loves me.

Moments pass between us without words.

"I love you," I blurt out.

I didn't mean to say it, but I don't regret it. My face is hot and my hands are numb from all the blood rushing to my chest.

Her smile doesn't falter as she says, "I know."

And we stand like that, staring at each other for countless seconds. The silence is heavy, but in a safe way. Sophie opens her mouth, but my mother's voice cuts through our moment.

"Carter! I think there's one in here!"

We break our gaze and I say, "I've got to go check on her."

Sophie nods and takes a step toward me. She puts her hand in mine and squeezes. Then she leaves.

I stretch my neck and silently walk into the living room to help my mother, my heart still pounding.

SOPHIE

Carter Jax loves me. Carter Jax loves me.

I know he loves me. And hearing him say it out loud makes my heart leap.

I walk to school, bouncing, because I can't seem to keep my feet on the ground.

I didn't say it back.

Why didn't I say it back?

I love him. More than anything. Why didn't I just tell him that?

I'm an idiot.

I'm an idiot with bouncing feet.

The school day drags on. It's seriously the longest day in the history of school. I'm impatient to get out. I'm going to run home and…do what, exactly?

Pound on Carter's door and declare my love?

No. I'll wait until the swing. I'll wait until we're swinging away our troubles and then I'll tell him.

School finally ends and I hurry home. I do homework and make dinner and wait impatiently for bedtime.

But it takes forever to get the Littles in bed.

Chloe's asking for a drink of water every fifteen minutes, Abram's whining about watching more TV, and Michael's throwing a fit about how he's almost a grown up.

"Listen, Michael, if you're referring to yourself as a 'grown up', then you're still totally a kid. 'Grown ups' call themselves adults."

My words are lost on Michael, so he storms into his room and shoves his earphones in.

I'm hurrying down the hall so I can get to the swing early when the phone rings. It's Carter.

"Hey, Sophie."

"Hey." I know what he's going to say. He only calls for one reason.

"My mom's freaking out so I've got to stay here tonight. Sorry." He sounds sorry.

My heart falls because I had this great proclaim-my-love plan.

"I'm sorry," I say. What I want to say is "I love you", but I don't. Because I'm a coward. "Can I help you at all?"

I can hear him smile. "No. But thanks."

We hang up and I feel lost. I pace around my house for an hour because my heart isn't settled. Something's wrong.

I'm wrong.

I feel…off. And sad.

Sad because the boy next door loves me and he doesn't know that I love him back.

I try to calm myself down and come up with a plan to trot over there in the morning with *I love Carter Jax* written on my forehead.

I turn out the lights and climb into my bed. My bed faces my window on purpose. I can see right into Carter's room. I always leave my window open because it makes me feel closer to him.

It seems like hours before I see Carter enter his room. He stares at my window. He can't see me, he doesn't know I'm awake, but he's staring anyway.

Because he loves me.

Eventually he turns out his light and collapses on his bed. I look at his darkened room for a long time before I realize I'm shaking.

My heart is pounding so hard I can see my chest hammering. Almost as if my heart is trying to reach across our yards and jump into Carter's body.

My pulse picks up even more and I sit up, realizing my restless heart won't make it through the night like this.

I get up and decide to sneak out of my house and tiptoe up to his window. I've seen this done on TV so I'm sure it's easy.

Instead of using my front door like a normal, sane, non love-crazy person would, I decide to actually climb out of my bedroom window.

The execution is more difficult than my love-struck brain had imagined.

For starters, the window screeches like a howling animal as I open it up far enough to fit my body through. Not exactly the stealth maneuver I was hoping for.

And the four foot drop to the earth below would have been much more pleasant had I been wearing shoes.

Did I think through the wardrobe thing? Of course not. I was too busy trying to keep my heart from leaping out of my chest and thudding over to Carter's room without my body.

So, no. I did not plan my sneaking-out outfit accordingly. Which is why I'm now standing, barefoot in the sticky mud beneath my window, wearing only a pair of gym shorts and a thin T-shirt with Snoopy on it.

The wind rustles through the big trees around our houses, momentarily deafening all sounds of the night as I look across the yard to where Carter's window sits shadowed in darkness. His room seems farther away than ever before for some reason, and I start to panic.

Not because the darkness is frightening and the shadows are moving of their own accord. But because I cannot wait another minute to tell Carter I love him.

So I make my way through our yards while the wind whips at my face and reminds me to grab a jacket the next time I decide to play Ninja Girl in the night.

The grass and gravel in between our windows is wet and cold on my bare feet as I step through the night, but I don't care. I'd walk on fiery coals if only to watch Carter sleep.

When I reach his window I notice it's open all the way, just like mine. It's probably been that way for years.

I'm not surprised.

But I'm moved.

We keep our windows open so we can hear each other, see each other, feel each other.

Because we love each other.

Thankfully, his window is low to the ground, making it easy for me to climb inside. I quietly place my feet inside his bedroom and wait for my eyes to adjust.

I see him sitting up in his bed.

He's awake and, from the crooked smile on his face, not surprised to see me. Probably because my squeaking windowpane woke him up.

So much for "sneaking" out.

I smile, mostly at myself for being so silly, but also because my heart is warm and happy now that I'm near Carter.

We don't say anything for a minute as whispering wind sails in from the window.

I slowly crawl onto his bed, dirty feet and all, and scoot over to where he is. He looks at me curiously, apprehensively. But still I say nothing.

I'm so nervous and happy and anxious and in love.

It's freaking me out—but in a good way.

I tuck my knees under me and look at him for a long time, which he let's me do without question.

"I love you too," I say without breaking our gaze.

My heart flutters.

"I know," he says, and slowly smiles.

My heart flies.

My world has just become whole.

CARTER

I've never been happier in my whole life. Sophie Hartman loves me.

I don't know what to do.

Do I kiss her?

Can I kiss her?

This is *Sophie*. She's the most important person in my life. I can't screw this up.

I reach over and take her hand in mine.

She smiles.

I look at our intertwined hands and warmth floods my heart. I lift her hand to my mouth and start to place soft kisses on her perfect, unscarred knuckles.

She's watching me, probably thinking I'm a moron.

Which I am.

But then she pulls her hand away from mine and a piece of me dies. I feel like I can't breathe and I'm pretty sure my heart has stopped.

But she smiles again.

"Carter," she says, and I hold my breath. "Please can I just..." She looks at me intently and bites her lip.

She's the most wonderful sight I've ever seen.

Then she kisses me. Not the big, sloppy kind of kiss you see in the movies.

No, she presses her lips to my eyebrow—the one with the scar from beer bottle.

Next she kisses the edge of my jaw—the one that was so swollen in the sixth grade I could only eat liquids.

Then the bridge of my nose—broken more times than I can count.

Then my chin—a steel-toed boot left that scar.

She just keeps kissing my scars. Every scar. She knows them all. She watched them all appear and heal.

"I never..." she says between kisses, "got to kiss your hurt away..." another kiss, "when we were little..." her lips move to my forehead, "and I always wanted to."

I might die of happiness.

Her lips move down to the corner of my mouth. The man who is my father split the crease open with a steak knife one night because he wanted to see me smile. It left a permanent white scar.

Her lips touch it gently.

Sophie's lips against mine make every punch, every kick, every wound, every scar worth it.

She pulls away from the corner of my mouth slightly and I'm perfectly still, afraid if I move I'll wake up.

Her breaths are warming my lips, my breaths are ragged and hot. She tilts her head to the side and looks at my mouth.

Then I kiss her.

In this moment, everything bad, everything painful, everything unfair disappears. It's just me and Sophie. Connected.

And I've never felt so whole.

SOPHIE

Three days later I'm sitting amongst my fellow classmates, all of us dressed in shiny robes, waiting to be called to the large podium set up under the basketball hoop in the gym.

Graduation day is here.

Other seniors seated around me are whispering and buzzing with excitement. Mr. Wesley is trying unsuccessfully to gain the attention of the restless crowd with a speech about "seizing the day" and "carving your own path" and "chasing your dreams."

The only dream I want to chase right now is the dream of getting out of this thick and heavy robe. My T-shirt and shorts underneath are sticking to my body, and my skin feels muggy and trapped beneath the suffocating material of the robe.

I really, really dislike the graduation gown.

The gym is filled with people, making the vaulted room hot and stuffy. Parents, siblings, and other miscellaneous family members line the walls and fill the bleachers. It's a pivotal day for most people.

Students around me are waving at loved ones in the crowd. Loved ones who've come to witness the oh-so-significant day of graduation.

There are no loved ones smiling down on me, however.

The Littles are in school and my mother (who is no longer my mother) probably doesn't even know what year it is, let alone that her eldest child is graduating high school today.

I'm not saddened by this. Just aware.

I look down the row of classmates seated next to me. Fifteen chairs away is Carter, stretching his neck and apathetically watching Mr. Wesley. He has no family members here for him either.

But he has me.

I look at his handsome face and tilt my head. He looks like a man today.

Not because of the robe—*definitely* not the robe. But because his face is filled with confidence and strength.

Today he looks…content.

And contentment looks good on him.

He looks down the row and our eyes meet. He smiles without hesitation, and I smile back like a giddy schoolgirl.

I love his guts.

The ceremony continues. Names are called. Diplomas are handed out and there is much rejoicing in the land, or whatever.

When the last name is called everyone throws their graduation cap into the air and cheers.

Well, almost everyone.

Carter and I spy one another and make our way towards each other.

Around us, proud parents are snapping pictures of their graduates and adorning them with flowers and hugs. The chaos is joyful and filled with hope and power. I'm happy for everyone around me. I'm slightly jealous of their faith in the future, but I genuinely hope they all "seize the day."

I reach Carter's side and look into his face. He smiles at me and tries to shove his hands in his pockets. The glossy robe is in his way, however, and his hands slide down its sleek fabric.

I laugh softly. "The robes suck."

"Yep," he smiles at me, "they do."

"Wanna ditch them?" I ask, half-joking, but he takes me up on it and unzips his, revealing faded jeans and a thin white T-shirt underneath.

I laugh again as I take my robe off as well and finally allow my skin and clothes to breathe. We drop our gowns on the gym floor, leave them there, and start walking toward the exit.

Carter breathes in deep. "So…we graduated."

I nod. "Yep."

"You feel any different?"

I look at him from the side. "Yeah…" my eyes fall to his lips. "But not because we graduated."

He eyes me as well. "Me too."

We keep walking.

Then, right in the middle of all our classmates—in the center of the crowded gym where teachers and parents and Whitneys and Evans are milling around—Carter reaches for my hand and holds it like it belongs to him.

Which it does.

I smile as we walk out of our graduation ceremony, connected.

CARTER

I did something sort of cheesy before graduation, and I'm sure Sophie's going to think it's stupid, but I don't care. I'm crazy about her and crazy people do crazy things.

We're walking hand-in-hand down the sidewalk toward our houses as the breeze blows. Sophie's teasing me about this-and-that as we chat about high school and teachers and subjects we hope we never have to study again.

It's normal.

It's wonderful.

My walk home from school has never been so happy.

We reach our houses and pause, hands still interlaced.

"Okay," I say, and of course, I sound like a moron, "I have a surprise for you...kind of. I mean, it's no big deal...I just...here, follow me."

Yep, total moron.

But Sophie smiles and plays along. She lets me lead her between our front yards and to the back, where the Big Oak stands guard over our houses and secrets.

Underneath the Big Oak, I've laid out a big blanket and set up a picnic. It's totally cheesy.

I'm sure Sophie's going to laugh at me, but she doesn't.

Not at first, anyway.

At first she just looks at me, tilts her hand to the side and smiles. *Then* she laughs. But not in a teasing way, in a happy way.

"I love it, I love it, I love it." Sophie's bouncing up and down and I feel victorious so I laugh right along with her.

We sit down and eat while we talk and sigh and laugh and sit in comfortable silence. When the food is gone and the sun is passing above us, we lay down, side-by-side on our backs, staring up at oak leafs and the sky.

Just like we did when we were little, except it's different now.

It's better.

Sophie's hand reaches across the blanket and wraps itself around mine.

We lay like that, staring up at the blue sky and the dancing leaves, for what seems like hours. We've never been to the Big Oak in the daytime before, and something about it is...promising.

For whatever reason it seems like today, this moment, underneath the Big Oak and the blue sky, is the beginning of something new and forever.

Sophie takes a deep breath and exhales slowly with a smile. "This is way better than running away to Hollywood."

I smile. "Totally."

I squeeze her hand to remind myself that I'm not dreaming. I'm in love with Sophie Hartman and it doesn't scare me at all.

SOPHIE

Two days later, the dull morning sun falls quietly upon the blackened remains of Carter's kitchen.

Our graduation picnic seems like an eternity ago.

I'm sitting cross-legged on the damaged kitchen floor praying the sound of my thudding heart doesn't disturb the silence I know Carter needs right now.

He's sitting next to me, staring off into nothing, and I feel completely useless.

I don't know what to do so I scoot closer to him.

A minute goes by.

I tuck my hair behind my ear and scoot even closer.

Another minute passes and the room feels cold.

I wiggle closer still until our knees are touching.

Much better.

I take a deep breath and wait out the silence.

CARTER

On graduation night my mom lit the kitchen on fire.

After Sophie and I finished our picnic we took her siblings to the school carnival. While we were there I got a phone call from the police and rushed to the hospital to find my mom with burn marks all over her body and stitches in her head.

She burned down two walls of our kitchen and shattered the kitchen window by throwing herself against it in a delusional rage.

She's bandaged and bruised, but she'll be okay.

Physically, at least.

The doctors insisted she be transferred to a mental healthcare hospital, undergo psychiatric evaluation, and be admitted as a resident—indefinitely.

The social workers were there also, assuring me she'd be happier and safer under the care of the state. I nodded because they wanted me to, but my stomach felt hollow.

I had no words or fight left inside me.

My mom seemed excited by the idea of leaving. Even yesterday, when they loaded her into the state van, she didn't look afraid. She smiled like she was going on a tropical vacation.

I didn't cry, but my heart hurt.

This is what the doctors have been saying would happen for years. I shouldn't be surprised. I should be happy she's finally surrounded by skilled individuals who can give her the kind of care she really needs.

I should feel good about this.

I should feel relieved.

I'm not.

I've been sitting on the floor of my burned kitchen for three hours. In silence.

Not mourning.

Not wallowing.

Just…shocked.

It's heavy in here.

Sophie's sitting next me though, helping to shoulder the weight. She hasn't said a word all morning. She doesn't need to.

I should be sad and full of despair. I should be black inside and empty.

But I'm not.

There's no darkness inside me.

Because Sophie is here.

And I can feel her goodness seeping into me.

It's rolling across the glass-littered floor and floating up the charred walls. It's drifting through the stale smoke and settling on my back, wrapping me in hope.

Hope for a new life, a new beginning.

For both me and my mother.

Hope for the future and gratefulness for what I have now.

Like Sophie.

"I love you," I say, not looking at her.

"I know." She shifts a little, her small knee brushing against mine. "I love you too."

"I know," I say and I reach out until my hand finds hers.

She kisses my knuckles and holds my hand like she means it.

And suddenly I'm okay.

We both are.

We sit in silence for who knows how long, just like that.

Knee-to-knee.

Hand-in-hand.

I hear Michael, Abram and Chloe's laughter coming from next door. They're messing around; oblivious, happy.

I smile. We'll all be okay.

Today...tomorrow. Everyday.

I turn to Sophie, stare at her for a minute, and ask, "Wanna just...get away? Start over?"

She looks at me and smiles. "Totally."

The heaviness in the room slowly lifts, filling the kitchen—and my chest—with hope.

SOPHIE

We'll be okay, me and Carter. We don't really have a plan but I know we'll be okay anyway. Because we have his beat up truck, three thousand dollars, and the Littles all packed up.

And we have love.

The real kind.

We're going to go somewhere. Somewhere far away from the hurt, but close enough to visit Mrs. Jax .

Me, Carter, and the Littles.

We'll be poor and have to work hard, and we'll probably fight and want to give up. But at the end of the day, we'll still have each other and that's all we need.

The Littles pile into the backseat of Carter's truck and buckle themselves in while I hop into the passenger seat and take a deep breath. The good kind of breath. The kind that fills you with hope and peace.

Carter jumps in and starts the engine. He's handsome today.

He's handsome everyday, but today he is my hero, so he's extra handsome.

He looks at me and smiles. A real smile. The kind of smile I've rarely seen over the years. I hope our new life brings him more of those smiles.

He grabs my hand, kisses it briefly, and smiles back at the Littles, "Ready for an adventure?"

Chloe shouts, "Whoo-hoo!" while the boys nod and try not to grin.

They're happy.

We're all happy.

Carter pulls out of the drive and I feel free.

We won't have much as we start this new life. But we'll have us. We'll have love. We'll have family….

I look in the back of the truck at all the stuff we've packed up, one thing in particular catching my eye.

…And we'll have the old porch swing. How can we be anything but happy with all that?

I breathe in deep, smell the ocean, and smile brighter than I ever have before as we drive away from Penrose Street.

Carter Jax has already made all my dreams come true.

And it's only the beginning.

Chelsea Fine

Don't miss Chelsea Fine's new series The Archers of Avalon, starting with

Read the first chapter now!

Prologue

She awoke with her face against cold, damp dirt. Morning sunlight cast a silent glow on the earth below and somewhere nearby a bird began to sing.

Dawn.

She looked across dirt and dead leaves at tall trees and wild shrubs swaying in the morning wind. She was in a forest.

A deserted and unfamiliar forest.

What the…?

Carefully she stood and canvassed the area, trying to make sense of her surroundings, but nothing triggered any memory as to why she'd slept in the woods. Nothing triggered any memory as to how she'd arrived there.

Nothing triggered any memory at all.

Her breathing became more rapid as she tried to remember. She scanned the forest desperately, her dark hair swinging around her head as she spun in circles and began to panic.

More birds were chirping now and the rising sun gave way to a shower of light, illuminating everything before her. Bright. Happy. Completely confusing.

She couldn't remember last night, or the night before, or the night before that…she couldn't remember anything.

Not her family, not her past. Nothing.

She rummaged through her brain for something—*any* information at all. But her memories seemed lost. Stolen, even. As if plucked with magical precision from her head leaving nothing but emptiness.

Terror began to set in.

She closed her eyes and tried to think. There had to be something in the emptiness; something inside her head that could echo back a memory. She scanned her mind desperately until finally….

Click.

Hidden far away, in the back of her brain, was a tiny scrap of knowledge. It flitted about like a hummingbird, teasing her with answers as she chased it around. When she finally grasped it, her eyes flew open with two revelations.

Her name was Scarlet Jacobs.

And she was fifteen years old.

Aside from that, she remembered nothing.

1

Two years later…

The third weekend in June was, to most people, a three-day stretch of summer. But to the townspeople of Avalon, Georgia, it was known as the Kissing Festival. For three weekend nights residents would gather in the town center for fun, food, and kissing.

Lots and lots of kissing.

It was tradition to greet your neighbor—or any other random stranger you came across—with a kiss. Sometimes these kisses were an innocent peck on the cheek and other times a passionate mouth-to-mouth embrace. Either way, it was difficult to spend an evening at the Kissing Festival without getting smooched. Which was why Scarlet wanted to go home.

She stood amidst the kissing chaos in the town square, waiting for Heather—her best friend and self-declared fashion consultant—to show up, while glancing around at the evening's festivities. Kissing booths, kissing workshops, kissing competitions…all across town the celebration was in full swing.

It was similar to a New Year's Eve party, but instead of mistletoe the townsfolk hung paper stars above their doorways. And instead of a single evening with champagne and confetti, there was an entire weekend with parades and, well, confetti.

Heather was late, which was no surprise, but Scarlet didn't like standing by herself in a crowd of tongue-happy citizens. Her fear of being kissed by some well-meaning neighbor was growing by the second.

She kicked at the sidewalk with a scuffed-up sneaker, trying to look uninterested as her blue eyes traced the familiar drawings she'd inked on the toes and sides of her shoes.

Scarlet had a tendency to doodle. She drew on her arms, her legs, her notebooks. But mostly she drew on her shoes. And she drew one thing in particular. A circular symbol with an arrowhead in the center.

It was the only memory—or rather, image—her broken mind had managed to retrieve since her "great awakening" in the woods two years ago. And it floated in and out of her dreams relentlessly.

Scarlet looked down at her feet where she'd drawn the mysterious symbol dozens of times. Surely it meant something. Surely her brain had salvaged the image for a reason. But Scarlet couldn't remember.

Which was the story of her life.

Her chest tightened as she thought back over the last twenty-seven months. The day she awoke in the outer forest of Avalon was the scariest day of her life. No fear could compare to the fear of the unknown. Especially when the unknown was *her*.

The days following her awakening were still a blur. Scarlet remembered hospitals, social workers, and police reports, but not clearly. The first clear memory she had was the day she met her guardian-to-be, Laura Walker.

Laura was an attractive young businesswoman who managed to get custody of Scarlet despite the many court hurdles associated with abandoned minors. She took Scarlet in, gave her a home, and tried to make her life as normal as possible.

But normal was wishful thinking.

Not knowing what existed in the past was like running through a maze blindfolded.

And that's how Scarlet had felt.

Blind and lost. Running through a dark labyrinth without direction, without purpose. She was a missing person whom no one missed, and all her unanswered questions kept her up at night, staring at the ceiling in fear and confusion.

Without Laura and Heather in her life, Scarlet probably would have gone crazy.

Laura had been compassionate and hopeful, always encouraging Scarlet not to give up on her past, believing she could still recover her memories. She gave her support and understanding without treating her like a broken doll in need of repair.

And Heather had kept Scarlet from sinking into depression and crying her eyes out every day. Heather was constantly dragging Scarlet out of bed and into the real world, trying to make her have "fun" and "be happy."

It was obnoxious.

And Scarlet loved her for it.

Heather had made it her mission to make Scarlet fully participate in life. So, here Scarlet was, attending the blasted Kissing Festival. "Participating in life." And where was Heather? Running late.

Scarlet watched the Main Street parade pass by. A float adorned with large papier-mâché lips cruised along as happy music filled the air and strangers kissed unabashedly beneath hanging stars—as if exchanging a kiss with your hair stylist and bank teller wasn't weird at all. Ick.

Glancing up, Scarlet spied a trio of paper stars hanging from a tree branch above her and quickly moved to a star-free spot on the sidewalk. Roving her eyes over the festivities, Scarlet's gaze caught on something. Or rather, someone.

Across the street, beyond the parade and chaos, stood a guy wearing a black T-shirt and baseball hat. The hat was pulled low over his eyes, making it impossible for Scarlet to see his face, but she could feel him staring at her.

Intently. Deliberately.

He tilted his head to the side and something deep within Scarlet began to stir.

The stirring started in the pit of her stomach, wove into her chest and wrapped itself around her heart; squeezing until her breaths became shallow and her heart began to hammer.

Weird.

Eyeing him more closely, Scarlet assumed he was her age, seventeen or so, if not a few years older. Tufts of dark hair peeked from beneath the hat he wore, but shadows made it impossible to see any facial features aside from his square jaw and full lips. Still, something about him seemed familiar.

Dangerous and safe and...*familiar*.

Who was he?

As if something were drawing her to him, Scarlet stepped forward and parted her lips—

"Phew!" Heather suddenly appeared at her side, out of breath and doubled over.

Blinking, Scarlet glanced at her best friend before immediately returning her gaze to the street. But the boy in black had vanished.

Scarlet's heart stopped pounding.

Heather righted herself. Her blonde hair was smoothed-down beneath a pink headband, matching her pink shirt and pink shoes. She wore a short jean skirt and a sleeve of shiny bracelets.

Even sweaty and panting, Heather looked perfect.

Scarlet looked down at her own outfit of shorts and an oversized green shirt and knew Heather would not be pleased.

Heather took fashion seriously.

Scarlet did not.

Sucking in air, Heather said, "Fluffy—Mrs. Allen's ferocious dog—chased me all the way down Pine Street trying to tear me to shreds with his razor fangs. I barely got away."

Scarlet scrunched her face. "Isn't Fluffy a Chihuahua?"

"Yes. A demon-possessed, human-eating Chihuahua."

"Sure."

As she caught her breath, Heather eyed Scarlet up and down, clearly forgetting about her near-death experience with the world's smallest breed of dog. "The baggy green shirt, Scarlet? Really?"

Scarlet rolled her eyes. "It's a kissing festival. Not a fashion festival."

"Well, thank God. Because you'd be booed out of Avalon." Heather ran a hand over her shiny hair. "I mean, seriously. You have a closet the size of a castle full of cute, appropriately-sized shirts, and you choose a parachute top for the Kissing Festival? Have you learned nothing from me?"

"I've learned not to go near Fluffy, the demon puppy from hell."

"I'm *telling* you, I almost died." Heather straightened her shoulders. "So who should we kiss first?" She puckered her heavily glossed lips as she looked around the town square.

The sun had dipped below the surrounding mountains, streaking the sky with the fading colors of dusk as street lamps started to click on. Tiny white lights strewn about the town began to shine against the falling shadows. Music in the air, twinkle lights in the sky, cobblestone streets and grassy knolls. It looked like a postcard.

Beside them, two senior citizens were tonguing each other under a set of stars.

A really gross, wet postcard.

"Uh...*you* can kiss whomever you'd like," Scarlet said as she began moving down Main Street, Heather at her side. "I'm only here for the free mouthwash."

The festival freebies were the only things Scarlet enjoyed about the event. Free toothpaste, free breath mints, free lip balm...it was like walking around inside an ad for the human mouth.

Heather tossed her blond hair over her shoulder with the kind of sass only pretty girls possessed. "No. You're here because you are fun and you really, really love kissing. Probably."

"Ha," Scarlet said. "I'm pretty sure I've never liked kissing random strangers."

Heather smiled. "Maybe we need to find you a hot stranger with yummy lips, just to be sure."

Strange lips? *Ew.* "Yeah. I'm all set on lips."

They walked past a makeshift dental booth advertising free deep cleanings. A balding man in white scrubs stood beside a dental chair, holding shiny exam instruments while he waved and smiled at people. If red paint were splattered about, it would have looked like a scene from a horror movie.

Heather smiled and waved at the bald man.

"Don't wave to the creepy dentist." Scarlet grabbed Heather's wrist.

"But I wave at everyone—oh look!" She nudged Scarlet's shoulder and nodded at a group of guys from school that were approaching with smiles—their attention primarily focused on Heather.

And why wouldn't it be? Heather looked like a giant piece of sexy bubblegum.

Scarlet, on the other hand, probably looked like a giant pea.

Flirty as always, Heather greeted each boy with double cheek kisses. *Intimate* cheek kisses, if ever there were such a thing. Leave it to Heather to make cheek-kissing inappropriate.

But then the boys proceeded to kiss Scarlet's cheeks as well and things got uncomfortable. After a series of bobbing heads and bonking noses, Scarlet was thoroughly embarrassed and completely grossed out.

The Kissing Festival. Worst idea ever.

After the boys moved on, Scarlet hastily wiped her cheeks while Heather sighed happily. "Don't you just love the Kissing Festival?"

Scarlet choked on a cough. "No. It's weird. And full of potential mouth diseases."

"Yeah, but you get to kiss guys like Aaron Jablonski," Heather said, staring after one of the departing boys.

Heather had tried to set Scarlet and Aaron up a few times last year, all with disastrous results.

Scarlet scrunched her nose. "He's not my type."

Heather rolled her eyes. "No one is your type. I keep trying to hook you up with these smoking hot guys and you just keep shutting them down. You're missing out on some fabulous opportunities."

"You mean like Aaron back there? The guy who kicked-off our first date by asking me how old my hot mom was? Yeah, golden opportunity he was."

"In his defense, your mom *is* hot and looks like she's twenty."

"That's because Laura's not my mom, she's my guardian, and she's only thirty. But that's not the point. The point is that I don't want to date anyone right now. The whole amnesia thing makes dating…just weird. And I don't feel like dealing with any of it right now."

Or ever.

Heather looked Scarlet over thoughtfully. "I understand that you're afraid to connect with other people. I just don't want you to use your mysterious past as an excuse not to live your life, you know? You can't just exist, Scarlet. You have to *live*." She stretched her arm out in front of a dozen kissing booths set up in the park and wagged her eyebrows. "And you have to *kiss*."

Scarlet stopped walking and glared at her friend. "No."

Twinkle lights draped back-and-forth between the tall trees in the park, making a canopy of stars above the red and pink kissing booths below. Behind the booths, a band was set up in a large white gazebo, playing love songs as couples danced in the grass.

It was like Valentine's Day.

On crack.

"Oh, come on, Scarlet." Heather scolded. "Be fun."

Scarlet shook her head. "I'm not paying someone to stick their tongue down my throat."

"They don't *French* kiss you." Heather smiled. "Unless you *want* them to." She wagged her eyebrows again.

Scarlet smiled. "I'm going to pass."

"Whatever." Heather straightened her hair, her bracelets jingling merrily. She sighed. "I guess I'll just have to go without you. But just so you know," she pointed at Scarlet with one perfectly manicured fingernail and used her best authoritative voice, "I will get you to kiss—and I mean *kiss*—a hot boy this weekend. It *will* happen and you *will* like it."

As she spun around and headed to the booths Scarlet smiled and called out, "Good luck with that."

Heather's only response was a flick of her hand.

Watching her friend walk away, Scarlet stood alone in the sea of kissing townsfolk and took a deep breath. The warmth and stickiness of the summer day still clung to the night air as Scarlet let her eyes roam across the park. Once again, her eyes caught on the black-shirted stranger and she felt the stirring come back to life in her chest.

What was it about this guy?

His gaze was focused on the festivities and not on Scarlet, so she had a moment to examine him privately. His face still hidden shadows, he stood with confidence, his broad chest held high with his arms crossed in front. The dark hair escaping his hat curled a bit around his neck and Scarlet felt a memory inside her begin to rustle.

Suffocated and imprisoned, it struggled to break free. She continued to stare at the stranger, hoping the memory would surface, when he suddenly turned in her direction. And although she couldn't see them, she was certain his eyes were fixed on hers.

Something about him was definitely familiar.

Scarlet's heart pounded and her mind started spinning. For a moment—for a wonderful split second—she felt as though she was close to unlocking the memory; that precious, lost treasure buried somewhere in the abyss of her mind. Her brain ticked and turned, roving her soul for something to grasp at.

It was there. She knew it. She could *feel* it. It was piecing itself together…almost a complete thought…

So close…so close—

Scarlet took a step forward. Maybe she would just walk over to him. Maybe she would introduce herself to him and see if he knew anything about her. She took a few more steps. Maybe if she got close enough to see his face clearly—

"Leaving so soon?" said a male voice behind her.

Scarlet froze. The voice at her back was familiar. Beautifully, impossibly familiar. Reminiscent, even. Almost perfect.

It was a voice from her past. A voice she *knew*.

What was the deal tonight? Why did everything seem so freaking familiar?

Scarlet pulled her eyes from the boy in black, turning to see the keeper of the familiar voice.

She didn't know him, which was disappointing. But he was gorgeous, which was not disappointing.

Wearing a blue shirt and a disarming smile, he looked to be a little older than Scarlet. His dark hair, square jaw, and brown eyes complimented the tan skin that wrapped around his broad frame.

He was smiling at her. Waiting.

Oh crap. What had he just said to her?

She blinked a few times. "What?"

His smile deepened, revealing two adorable dimples as he took a step toward her. "You looked like you were about to leave."

Scarlet looked over to where the boy in black had been but, once again, he'd disappeared, taking any hope Scarlet had of recovering a memory with him. Her pounding heart sank in her chest.

She turned back to the hot guy in the blue shirt and smiled tightly. "Nope. I wasn't leaving."

"Well, in that case," he said, holding out his hand, "I'm Gabriel Archer. Kissing Festival virgin."

Gabriel Archer.

Scarlet tilted her head to the side, wishing his name meant something to her in the same way his musical voice had.

But no.

She smiled as she took his hand, both grateful and disappointed he chose to greet her with a handshake instead of a kiss—*what is wrong with me?* "I'm Scarlet Jacobs. Kissing Festival protester."

"I like you already." He smiled as they ended their handshake.

She tucked her lips in and pressed down, suddenly rethinking the baggy green shirt.

With a smile, Gabriel shoved his hands into the pockets of his perfectly fitting jeans. "So why do you protest? Too many guys to fend off?"

"Uh, no. It's not the 'guys' I'm worried about. It's the whole town. Everyone is so..." Scarlet tried to think of a nicer word than *insane*.

"Happy? In love?"

"*Yes*. It's so weird," Scarlet said. "I came last year, and vowed never to return again. But my best friend shamelessly begged me to come and I totally caved. And now I'm surrounded by," Scarlet gestured to the crowd in the park, "all these love-sick goobers."

Gabriel laughed. "Yeah, I hate love-sick goobers. They're so happy and annoying and *pleasant*...always trying to be nice and friendly." He rolled his eyes. "It's *so* irritating."

Scarlet smiled. "Shut up."

"Why did you vow never to return? Was it the dentist guy? Because that's completely understandable."

"He's creepy, right?"

"Totally." Gabriel gave a fake shudder, making her laugh.

She smiled to herself. Something about this guy made her feel comfortable. And his voice was just heavenly, singing to her soul like she knew him.

She answered, "No, actually, I didn't want to come back because last year I watched the kissing relay games and nearly threw up. That's why I tried my very hardest to stay at home tonight."

"And when you say your 'very hardest', you're referring to your complete lack of resolve when caving to your best friend, correct?"

Scarlet nodded. "Precisely."

He smiled and looked around. "Where's this conniving best friend of yours? I'd like to congratulate her on suckering you into attending this absurd festival of love and happiness."

Scarlet pointed to where Heather stood in line at one of the many kissing booths.

"Ah," he said, nodding. "She looks like a happy lovesick goober."

"Oh, she is."

Heather *was* happy. Happy and bubbly and excited about everything. And beautiful in that Miss America way every girl envied. She was nothing like Scarlet.

Heather was loud, outgoing, fashion-savvy, and girly.

While Scarlet was quiet, sarcastic, not interested in jewelry and dressed like a boy.

But their friendship worked. As different as they were, Scarlet felt more bonded to Heather than anyone else she'd met since waking up in Avalon because Heather had accepted Scarlet—amnesia and all.

They'd met two summers ago at the mall, a few weeks before sophomore year began. Laura had taken Scarlet to buy a new wardrobe—since Scarlet's slumber party in the woods hadn't exactly come with a closet full of clothes—and had left Scarlet in charge of picking out her own attire.

Shopping nearby, Heather had seen Scarlet eyeing a pair of unflattering jeans and had immediately interjected herself into Scarlet's life as her personal shopper. Soon after they became close friends.

When Scarlet first told Heather about her amnesia, Heather had freaked out.

Not in the expected O-M-G-you're-a-weirdo kind of way, but in an O-M-G-this-sounds-like-a-movie way.

She spent months talking nonstop about finding Scarlet's parents, starting a 'Who is Scarlet Jacobs' fund, and doing DNA testing to see if Scarlet was from a different planet.

It was obnoxious.

Sweet, in an overbearing, obsessive-friend way, but obnoxious.

Heather thought it was "cool" Scarlet didn't have a past. She was convinced Scarlet had been a government spy who'd had her memory erased in order to ensure the safety of the world. Because Heather was a drama queen.

But it was easier for Scarlet to play along with Heather's ridiculous government theory than it had been to wallow in self-pity. Heather had been a welcome distraction.

In a way, she'd saved Scarlet's life. Or at least, her emotional well-being. She'd given Scarlet something to laugh about and a friendship to believe in. She'd given Scarlet hope.

She was bright and sunny and full of positivity. Sometimes it was annoying, but most of the time, Scarlet needed it. She valued Heather's role in her life and respected her a great deal.

Even though, at that very moment, Heather was paying to kiss a boy.

"Yeah," Scarlet watched Heather apply more lip gloss at the kissing booth. "She is definitely happy."

A moment of silence hung between them and Scarlet shuffled her feet. "So, this is your first Kissing Festival?"

He ran a hand through his dark hair. "Yeah."

"What do you think?"

"Honestly?" He gave a crooked smile and shrugged. "I think it's…charming."

"Charming?"

Not the word Scarlet would have chosen.

He nodded as he looked around the park. "Yeah, it's…I don't know, nice. Everyone being friendly and positive. People dancing and laughing. It's refreshing. Sometimes the world is a cold place but this…this is nice."

Scarlet wrinkled her brow. "I guess so…" She looked around at some of the happy couples nearby; whispering in each other's ears, playfully kissing beneath paper stars, sharing lip-shaped popsicles. "It's sorta...pleasant. All the love and flirting."

She leaned to the right, accidently brushing arms with Gabriel, and her insides sparked at his touch. Blushing, she immediately repositioned herself so there was space between them.

They watched the park crowd without speaking as Scarlet waited for her cheeks to cool. Was she totally crushing on a stranger? Yep.

Gabriel grinned at her. "So what's your story, Scarlet?"

She inhaled deeply, thinking of where to start.

Well, two years ago I was abandoned in a forest outside of town and then taken into custody by this pretty woman named Laura, who gave me a home so I could have a normal life and go to high school. Oh, and I have amnesia. You know. Same ol', same ol'.

Yeah, probably not the best way to keep Gabriel around. Instead, Scarlet decided to go with the random-facts-about-yourself answer.

"Well, I speak Spanish," she said.

One of the few perks of having amnesia was that, every once in a while, Scarlet would uncover a hidden talent. Like Spanish.

"Also," Scarlet continued, "I'll be a senior at Avalon High this year. And I love ice cream. What's your story?"

He laughed. "Long and complicated. But the short answer is I just moved here from New York, I don't like snakes, but I do like this festival."

Scarlet nodded. "Because of all the love and positivity and goobers?"

He shrugged. "Among other things."

His brown eyes slanted to her and Scarlet felt her face warm again. What the crap? Since when was she a blusher?

Scarlet was suddenly very aware of how close they stood to one another and, looking up, caught sight of a cluster of paper stars dangling from the tree above. Something akin to panic shot through her.

Why did Georgia have to have so many trees?

Paper stars were *everywhere*.

Her heart began to race at the thought of Gabriel kissing her. Half of her wanted him to, but the other half—the sane, logical, you-don't-like-to-kiss-strangers half—wanted to flee from the park and burn down every tree in Georgia.

Her eyes fell from the stars down to Gabriel's mouth and quickly back up to his eyes.

He looked up, noticed the stars, and tilted his head. "Do you think it's weird to kiss someone you barely know?"

No, it's perfectly normal and gives us a fantastic excuse to make out. Kiss me!

"Totally weird," she said, immediately wanting to slap herself.

He nodded. "Me too."

Scarlet's hypocritical heart sank.

He flashed his dimples. "I guess now I've got a good reason to get to know you, don't I?"

Scarlet narrowed her eyes. "Who said I'd let you kiss me even if you got to know me?"

He nodded his head with a smile. "Challenge accepted."

"I'm baaaaack!" Heather rushed up to Scarlet, completely unaware of Gabriel. "I came, I kissed, I conquered. Now let's go find you a hot guy with a tasty mouth." She reached for Scarlet's arm, saw Gabriel, and froze.

Her mouth hung open for a moment as she took him in. "*Or*...." She looked Gabriel up and down shamelessly. "We could just stay here and talk to this lovely gentleman."

Heather whipped her head around and shot Scarlet an *O-M-G-who-is-this-hottie?* look.

Scarlet cleared her throat. "Heather, this is Gabriel. Gabriel, Heather."

Heather put on her best smile and turned to Gabriel. "Why, hello Gabriel. It's nice to meet you."

Dimples showing, Gabriel said, "You too, Heather."

"Are you new to Avalon? I've lived here all my life and I don't think I've ever seen you before. I'm sure I'd remember." She may as well have batted her lashes for all the flirt dripping from her tongue.

"Yes. I just moved here from New York." Gabriel smiled, his eyes sliding to Scarlet.

"Well then, welcome to Avalon. And welcome to the Kissing Festival." Heather went up on her tiptoes and gave Gabriel a kiss on each cheek. "So what brought you to Avalon?"

He paused. "Family business."

"What kind of business?"

"History."

"What kind of history?"

Scarlet glared at her nosey best friend.

Gabriel cleared his throat. "Just, you know, general history."

Heather narrowed her perfectly shadowed eyes at him. "Your family is in the business of *general history?* Wow. That's weird. And vague."

"Heather," Scarlet shot her a warning look. "Be cool."

With an exhale, Heather straightened her shoulders and smiled. "So, Gabriel. Would you like to come watch the kissing relays with us?" She rubbed her hands together like sweating people kissing in between sprints wasn't disgusting.

"You should come," Scarlet said, hoping Heather hadn't scared him off. "I might throw up. It'll be fun."

He laughed. "As much as I would love to watch you vomit, I can't. I have to go."

Scarlet nodded pleasantly despite the disappointment she felt.

"Will you be here tomorrow night?" Heather asked.

Gabriel looked at Scarlet for a moment and said, "Yes. Yes, I will."

"Fantastic. We'll see you tomorrow then." Heather kissed Gabriel's cheeks goodbye.

"It was nice to meet you, Heather," Gabriel said. He smiled at Scarlet. "Goodbye, Scarlet Jacobs."

"Goodbye," she said as Gabriel disappeared into the crowd of kissers, even though she wanted to shout, *Don't leave. You make me feel normal.*

Not two seconds passed before Heather turned to Scarlet with her mouth hanging open. "O-M-G, Scarlet. *W-T-F?*"

Heather actually spoke in text language. It took Scarlet a long time to get used to this—mostly because Scarlet had to *learn* text lingo in order to decipher conversations with Heather. Sure, Scarlet woke up in the woods with a complete understanding of the Spanish language...but 'LOL'? Nothing.

"Don't W-T-F me," Scarlet snapped. "What about W-T-F *you*? What was with the interrogation back there?"

She shrugged innocently. "I like getting to know hot guys. Especially hot guys who are chatting it up with my best friend at the Kissing Festival." Heather looked over her shoulder at where Gabriel had disappeared. "Where did you find him?"

"Find him? He's not a cereal toy, Heather."

"No—but ooh! How awesome would that be? You open a box of Trix and *wham!* Out pops a hot guy. I would *so* eat more cereal." Heather looked back at Scarlet with excitement in her eyes. "He's gorgeous. Like Greek-god-gorgeous. Did you guys kiss?"

"No."

"Lame."

"I know."

"Tomorrow," Heather said. "Tomorrow, I will make sure you two kiss. And I will also be in charge of your outfit. You clearly cannot be trusted to dress yourself."

"Stop hating on my shirt."

"It's not a shirt, it's a curtain. You look like a bad set of drapes from the 70s. Okay." Heather took a deep breath and gave Scarlet a crooked smile. "Time to go watch grown-ups run laps and pass the baton of saliva."

Wonderful. Let the retching begin.

Scarlet mocked a gag, but followed her friend through the crowd anyway. Meeting Gabriel had put Scarlet in a better mood. She almost didn't hate the festival anymore. Almost.

Just as they left the grassy park, Scarlet caught sight of her mystery boy-in-black again. He was farther away this time but she could tell he was still looking at her. Scarlet's heart started to thrum again as her mind sparked with the promise of a memory.

She slowed her steps to eye him more clearly, but a group of people passed in front of her, blocking her view. And when the crowd cleared he was nowhere to be found.

Scarlet stretched her gaze across the park as far as she could but found nothing. He'd been there one moment and was gone the next.

Just like the memory.

****

Familiar pain gradually reentered Tristan's veins as he drove away from the festival—away from Scarlet—and tugged on the collar of his black shirt, adjusting to the chronic ache he suffered without her.

Tonight had been an accident; seeing Scarlet….feeling her so close to him. Had he known she'd be at the festival, he never would have gone.

He'd almost gotten used to the grief that wracked his body in her absence; almost learned to live with it. But tonight had undone any hope he had of peace without her.

Tristan rubbed the back of his neck as his green eyes stared at the dark Georgia road ahead of him.

Long ago, he'd been cursed with a fever of desperation.

Nonstop, unrelenting desperation.

Bursting from his heart two years ago, it had taken him by the soul and wrung his insides dry with need. A need so impossible, so all-consuming, he could not deny it. And he could not silence it.

The sound of his soul, crying out for Scarlet, was deafening. Two years ago, the summons had started as a murmur; soft, faint and gentle, but over time it grew into a scream; bleating out in need and resonating in his chest without reprieve.

It was the sound of Scarlet's heart, alive and awake, beating steadily inside her chest, and echoing in his. Haunting him. Like a call. A ruthless demand to find her—to be with her.

He'd resisted the siren for years. And it nearly drove him mad.

Scarlet's heart calling to him, begging him.

Like it always did.

And he had broken down and answered.

Like he always did.

He had come to Avalon. Close enough to ease the fever. Close enough to quiet his screaming heart. But distant enough to maintain his sanity.

Until tonight.

His accidental nearness to Scarlet at the festival had eased his torment, but filled him with a longing he couldn't indulge. And Gabriel had talked to Scarlet tonight, which was only going to make things worse. Tristan was pissed.

He drove into the thick woods outside Avalon and made his way to the large cabin he shared with his brother.

The cabin sat upon twenty acres of forestland and had a main floor, a basement, and an upstairs. The main floor held the kitchen, a living room, the den, and an office. The upstairs and basement were identical in layout; each with a sitting room, master suite, and a spare bedroom.

The upstairs belonged to Gabriel and the basement belonged to Tristan. They didn't like living together, but it was necessary. For now.

When he reached the cabin, Tristan exited his car with fury in his veins and slammed the front door behind him as he entered the cabin. He found his brother in the living room.

"What the *hell* Gabriel?"

Gabriel, who'd been searching for the remote control under the couch cushions, looked up at his brother. "What?"

"You talked to Scarlet tonight? Are you insane?" Tristan couldn't keep the panic out of his voice.

"Are you spying on me now?" Gabriel went back to his hunt. "That's disturbing."

"You messed up the plan, Gabe." Tristan bored his green eyes into his brother. "You agreed not to meet her until the curse was broken." He started pacing the living room, fear and nervousness coiling inside him.

It was happening again.

The pain…the brokenness…the death….

This was the beginning of the end.

Gabriel said, "I had to see her, Tristan. I just wanted to talk to her and make sure she was okay. And I didn't feel like waiting around another few years while you *tried* to break the curse. Your plan—which is totally evil, by the way—isn't working."

"My plan isn't evil. It's necessary. And it will work."

Giving up his search for the control, Gabriel stood. "Your plan is completely evil. You're trying to murder someone."

Tristan stopped pacing. "I'm trying to save Scarlet's life. It's the only option we have."

Gabriel rolled his eyes. "No, it's not."

"We don't have time to chase after a legend, Gabe. Scarlet is going to *die*." He swallowed, tempering the emotion that coated his voice. "My plan is the only way to save her."

Gabriel threw his hands in the air. "Your plan is murder."

"It's not like I'm butchering an innocent lamb."

"Well, how would I know that?" Gabriel shrugged. "You haven't exactly been forthcoming with your victim's identity. For all I know, you're out hunting a sweet, little old lady."

Tristan stretched his neck.

Now that he was miles away from Scarlet, his physical pain had intensified; a constant reminder that he was, and always would be, without her.

"I'm not killing little old ladies," Tristan said.

"It's slaughter."

"It's not slaughter. I'm simply taking a life so Scarlet can keeps hers."

Out loud, it did sound bad.

But Tristan would do anything to save Scarlet.

Anything.

"Yeah, well…that doesn't make it any less wrong." Gabriel went back to searching for the control as silence fell between them.

Tristan exhaled. He needed more time to execute his plan and break the curse. And he needed Gabriel to stay away from Scarlet.

Tristan rubbed the back of his neck. "You were reckless tonight. Scarlet could have remembered who you were. She could have remembered who *I* was."

Gabriel shrugged. "She didn't."

"You can't see her again." Tristan's heart started pounding in fear. If Scarlet remembered him, if she came looking for him….

No. He couldn't let that happen.

Gabriel found the control and set it on an end table. "I've waited two years to 'meet' Scarlet and I don't want to leave her. I miss her."

"So do I, Gabe." Tristan shoved his hands in his hair. "But you don't see me running after her. You can't stay in her life. What if she remembers everything? Scarlet can't ever know about me—or meet me. It's too risky."

"Would you calm down?" Gabriel scowled. "I'm not going to tell her who she is until the curse is broken and I'm certainly not going to introduce her to you. So stop being so dramatic. And quit following me around town. That's weird."

"I wasn't following you," Tristan said. "I was meeting a client at the festival and I happened to see you."

Gabriel raised his eyebrows. "A 'client'? You mean hit man?"

Tristan didn't answer. He knew Gabriel didn't approve of his methods, but he didn't have time to look for less-gruesome ways to break the curse. He needed to save Scarlet.

"What's the matter?" Gabriel waved his hands sarcastically. "Big, mean Tristan can't commit murder all by himself?"

Tristan sneered, "I understand you don't like my plan, but don't act so righteous. My plan just might give you the happily ever after you've wanted for so long."

Gabriel made a face of disgust. "What, am I supposed to be grateful that you're willing to kill someone? Murder doesn't make you brave, Tristan. It makes you desperate."

"I *am* desperate."

Desperate to be free of the torment that tore at his soul day after day, begging for Scarlet. Desperate for peace.

Gabriel shook his head. "You're desperate and you're heartless."

Tristan laughed softly, his heart kicking at the irony of Gabriel's words. "Don't I wish."

Maybe if Tristan didn't have a heart, the pain and longing that plagued him wouldn't be quite as unbearable. Maybe if he didn't have a heart, he could get some sleep at night. But Tristan had a heart, and it was currently throbbing in pain because Scarlet was far away.

Gabriel shook his head. "Whatever. Just keep your evil heart away from me and Scarlet."

Tristan flexed a muscle in his jaw.

Gabriel knew nothing about Tristan's heart, evil or otherwise. It was the best—and worst—part of their relationship.

Gabriel would get to see Scarlet. Talk to her. Love her….

It would happen. Tristan couldn't stop it. And, if he really cared about Scarlet, he shouldn't stop it. But that didn't make the thought of them together any less gut-wrenching.

Tristan stared blankly at the floor as a piece of his heart broke.

His very real, very existent heart.

And so it begins.

Bugg Photographer LLC

Chelsea Fine grew up (and still lives) in the Phoenix, AZ area where she studied Design at Arizona State University. During college, she also took her first creative writing class, which is how she fell in love with writing. In 2007 while working at a credit union, she found herself staring at a computer screen and bored out of her mind. She promptly opened up a Word document and began writing a story to kill time (she knows she was a terrible employee!). Eight pages and forty-five minutes later, she realized she was having fun. Now, years later (after quitting the credit union, since she wasn't very good at "being on the clock"), she published her first novel *Sophie & Carter*. When she isn't working on her latest novel, she's an avid reader, a lover of music, a Battlestar Galactica fan, a coffee addict, a chronic texter, an obsessive teeth brusher, and a shameless superhero enthusiast.

Made in the USA
Lexington, KY
05 June 2013